LOST AND FOUND BY THE DUKE

THE RELUCTANT LORDS
BOOK ONE

ANDIE JAMES

D AND G BOOKS LLC

Cover design by Erin Dameron-Hill

Developmental editing by Jennifer Prokop

Copyediting by Nicholas Shea

ISBN 979-8-9884963-0-4

❀ Created with Vellum

CONTENTS

For my Mom. I love you, and I miss you.

CHAPTER 1

Kent, England—July 1819

Grace knew attending the house party would be a mistake, which was confirmed when she found herself pinned against a bookshelf in the back of the library, struggling to get away from the hostess's inebriated brother.

"Thomas, please, you're drunk," Grace implored. "You've known me since I was fifteen years old, and I know you will regret this in the morning," she said, adopting an amiable tone in hopes of making her appeal seem reasonable and slowing his impending figure.

She felt a hard and unrelenting pressure as the shelf bit into her hip. Thomas had cornered her into the back of the library after discovering her there, and his body was now uncomfortably close. Leaning heavily over her, he forced her further into the bookcase than she thought possible. She was certain to have a bruise on her hip in the morning.

The reasonable element of the negotiation tactics she had been trying to employ quickly became less viable with each second as Thomas continued to creep even closer, causing Grace to shiver in revulsion as the buttons of his waistcoat pressed into her stomach one by one. The smell of whiskey was evident on his breath, and she tried to repress a further shudder when the fine hairs on her temple stirred from a puff of air as he exhaled. "You weren't this pretty when you were fifteen," he slurred into her ear.

Grace berated herself for being in this position in the first place. It had been foolish to accept the invitation to the house party when she was already in a precarious social position, but desperate people tended to make impractical decisions. Being unable to sleep in an unfamiliar room and unsettled by her poor choices, she headed down to the library for a book.

Usually, reading helped Grace quiet and focus her mind so she might be able to get some rest. She had rationalized that with the house still mostly empty, having arrived a day before many of the guests, it was not too great a risk to wander downstairs. Now, looking into the half-lidded eyes of the young man she had not seen in close to a decade, she feared her decision to ignore propriety by walking around in her night clothes could make her situation even worse.

Grace wondered what had happened to Thomas in the intervening years that would make him act in such a manner. His expression, unfocused as it was, contained a contradictory mix of lust and derision. It was as if she, being a woman, was so far beneath him as to not be worth his notice—yet he still desired her.

"Thomas, stop this," Grace beseeched once more. She hated how her voice was beginning to tremble, making her sound weak. Just when she feared the situation was nearing a point of no return, Grace felt Thomas's movements stutter and then halt. He stiffened infinitesimally. Before she knew what was happening, a hand appeared on his shoulder, gripping firmly.

"I believe the lady asked you to stop," a voice said from behind Thomas. Grace could not see the man who had spoken, but his voice had been low and controlled, making it feel like a command that would be dangerous for Thomas to ignore.

"And who the hell are you?" Thomas spat with a sneer, turning to face the stranger.

"Henry Ellison, the fifth Duke of Carrington," the stranger replied coolly.

Thomas released her with a start, eyes widening as the gravity of this declaration and its icy delivery bore down on him. And Grace, free of his grip, could now see the duke with his cutting glare and clenched jaw directed at Thomas.

"I didn't know you had arrived, Your Grace. I was just having a little fun," Thomas replied with a laugh, failing to lighten the tension. "Catching up with an old friend of the family. Haven't seen Grace in years and wanted to let her know how much we missed her," he continued, unable to mask his slurred speech.

"Perhaps it might be best to share how much you missed her in the morning, when everyone is refreshed and has a clear head, don't you think?" Carrington was still calm but had taken command of the situation, his gaze never wavering from Thomas, who was wilting under the pressure like a flower in full July sunlight.

While the duke had yet to glance at Grace, she felt his protection acutely and was thankful he had intervened, though she resented being unable to control the situation on her own. It was apparent from Thomas's actions thus far that he respected the power of a duke far more than the protests of a woman.

Grace recalled that, even as a young man, Thomas shared his father's belief in the social structure of the aristocracy. They had kowtowed to those above them in the peerage, attempting to earn favor and bolster their own social standing among the *ton*. As a second son to a baron, even at the tender age of thirteen when she first met him, Thomas clearly demonstrated he felt himself lacking; Grace was sure he would do anything to increase his standing in the eyes of those he esteemed.

The sad reality was that Grace needed the duke's intervention, as much as she hated relying on others. There were a few women within polite society who had the power to use their influence within the *ton*, but Grace was not one of them. And with an elite nobleman now standing up for her, Thomas had no option other than to retreat.

"Of course, Your Grace. Tomorrow would be a much more hospitable setting for renewing acquaintances," Thomas acquiesced. "Can I help you find something here in the library to make your stay more comfortable?" he asked with a touch of desperation.

"No," Carrington said. "I believe it would be best if everyone called it a night. I will see you again in the morning, sir," he said with finality.

Having been dismissed, Thomas bowed his head with a look of unease before backing out of the room.

Still somewhat shaken, Grace slowly straightened away from the bookcase and attempted to compose herself. Now that Thomas was gone, a wave of embarrassment began to engulf her. She could feel the heat creeping up her neck and onto her cheeks as she began to blush, an unfortunate and frequent reaction of hers, and found she could not bring herself to look directly at the duke, even though she wanted to thank him.

"Are you alright?" Carrington asked softly, not wishing to further agitate her.

At his gentle tone, Grace was appalled to feel tears forming and knew she would need to leave soon to avoid crying in front of him. Carrington's kindness, a sentiment she was no longer used to receiving, would surely be her undoing, so with downcast eyes, she whispered, "Yes. I am well. Thank you, Your Grace."

"Are you injured? Is there someone I can get for you?"

The thought of bringing anyone else into the situation made Grace's pulse quicken. The last thing she needed was for word of this to spread. Raising her eyes to the duke, she implored, "No, please, I am well. I do not need anyone. I just need rest. I'll be on my way." He must have seen the anxiety in her eyes because he did not press her further.

Holding his gaze, fully seeing him for the first time, Grace had to catch her breath. He had kind, deep-gray eyes and chestnut hair that waved across his forehead, with stubble accentuating his perfectly angled jaw. Though he was one of the handsomest men she had seen in a long time, it was his demeanor that transfixed her: his forehead was creased out of concern for her well-being, and while he was much taller than her, he was not intimidating, his stance having softened with Thomas's departure. She felt safe in his presence, even when considering what had just transpired with Thomas, as well as her general unease around titled men.

"Very well," he said, eyes searching her own to discern her truthfulness. "If you are certain you're unharmed, I will see you to your room and make sure you remain undisturbed."

Wishing to escape the foreign and unsettling effect of his kindness, she protested, "I assure you, Your Grace, I am fine to make my own way back. I apologize for inconveniencing you this evening, but I am grateful for your assistance." Turning quickly, Grace fled the library and, terrified for her reputation, rushed back upstairs before anyone in the house could stumble upon them. Being found after hours and underdressed in the company of not one but two men could ruin her.

CHAPTER 2

Waking slowly and fighting sleep-heavy lids, Henry caught a glimpse of unfamiliar surroundings and was momentarily confused as to where he was. As sunlight pierced through the curtains and birds chirped in a nearby tree, his consciousness began to set in. With a groan, he remembered he was at Fitz's country home, Geffen House. While he normally enjoyed relaxing with Fitz and his family, this occasion was for Fitz's wife's house party. Henry adored Moira and would do almost anything for her, but attending this party was stretching the limits of his good grace.

Henry was more than prepared for a trying and tedious week. Still adjusting to the fact that he was now a duke, which was preceded by the unexpected deaths of his cousin and father in quick succession, he found the transition into polite society after leaving mourning straining. The way people now looked at him and deferred to his judgment based on a label was disconcerting. Henry had not changed; however, the new title made others regard him in a different light, lending his words a weight he was unused to. Who he was and what he did suddenly mattered, and that left him feeling insecure.

Henry knew this week others at the party would treat him differently than they had before, and he was not prepared for it. Even Moira's brother, Thomas— who had never treated him as anything special— deferred to Henry after hearing his new title last evening. It was the first time he had used his newfound clout to try and influence the actions of others, and while Henry was grateful it had worked given the situation, the quick deference had been unsettling.

Henry shuddered thinking about the young woman that Thomas had trapped in the library. He hoped she was alright after the unfortunate encounter and was glad he arrived when he did. Henry found Thomas's attitude toward women reprehensible. He hated how easy it was for men to disrespect and disregard women in their society due to the established and unspoken rules of the aristocracy. Henry respected the role women played in running homes and social spaces and felt they should be treated with the utmost care. Maybe this was an area where he could try and use his newly elevated status to sway opinions for the greater good.

Stretching, Henry allowed himself one final moment to luxuriate in the warmth of the bed linens before rising. He seemed to have slept later than usual, but then again, he had arrived late the evening before and had to break up the troubling scene in the library. He realized he did not actually know who the woman was and wondered about her connection to Fitz and Moira. While a bit timid last evening, which was understandable given the circumstances, she still made an impression on him. He would need to ask Fitz about her at breakfast. With that thought, Henry heard a perfunctory knock on his door before Smyth, his valet, promptly entered the room to assist with his morning ablutions.

"Good morning, Your Grace," Smyth greeted, all business, as he bustled toward the small dressing room holding a freshly pressed green jacket.

"Good morning, Smyth. Any worthy news this morning?" Henry asked, still abed.

"The chatter below is that most of the guests will arrive today and the party will commence officially this evening with dinner," Smyth answered in a muffled voice, responding from the adjoining room. "Captain Claybourn has seemingly been held up with final government business in London as the legislative session closes but should be here in the afternoon, and Mr. Bright will join from Ravenswood next door." Henry appreciated that Smyth mentioned the arrival of his friends, Reid and Sidney, as he would need their support to get through this party. It would be quite the week navigating mamas of the *ton*, who were anxious for their unmarried daughters to make the acquaintance of a new and unattached duke. Just the thought made him want to stay in bed forever.

Groaning, Henry got up and made his way over to the dressing room to watch his valet at work. "Smyth," Henry addressed him, leaning against the doorframe, "I don't think I'm going to make it through this week, I feel like an utter imposter."

"That's what I'm here for, Your Grace," Smyth replied. "I will make sure you look every inch the part of a duke and you will have one less thing to be anxious about."

Making sure the duke was turned out in a manner respectable to his rank brought Smyth great pride, and he was working valiantly to try and educate Henry on such matters. Smyth firmly believed that clothes made the man. He hoped that draping Henry in finery could help him gain the confidence needed to succeed in his newly elevated position. But Henry felt too stiff and buttoned up as he stared at himself in the mirror—like he was wearing the costume of a duke. And he suspected that until he felt comfortable in the finery, any efforts to feign a level of gravitas through his appearance would be severely undermined. Sensing his unease, Smyth let out a sigh.

Even a year later, Henry still found it odd to have assistance with a morning routine that he had been doing for the past thirty-six years before becoming a duke. But this morning he welcomed Smyth's help, as it allowed his mind to wander. This week would be a debut of sorts, as it had been fifteen years since he was an active member of high society, since before he enlisted in the army to halt the progress of Napoleon's forces. While Henry had been working in the war department's London office for the past few years, he had been too occupied to participate in polite society. If Henry had a failing, it was that he hated to do anything imperfectly, and he was still learning how to be a duke in society, so he supposed a few nerves about the house party were justified. But first he needed to find breakfast. The loud rumble of his stomach concurring as he finished buttoning his waistcoat.

"Thank you, Smyth. I believe I am set for the day. I will call you if I need to change for any of the activities later today."

"As you wish, Your Grace," Smyth said with a small bow before leaving the room. Henry shook his head at Smyth's deferential gesture; he did not think he would ever become accustomed to such attendance. His Aunt Hester had insisted that he needed to honor the family name and legacy by maintaining the dignity of the dukedom. Scared about stepping out of place and letting her down, he had learned to appreciate the service of those who attended him and helped him keep up appearances. So, Smyth stayed, though Henry felt what he provided was frivolous. He also did not wish to put the man out of a job. More than any other of his inherited responsibilities, Henry felt the weight of providing for those who relied upon his estate and holdings for their livelihood. And on that weighty note, he took a deep breath to prepare himself for the week ahead and walked downstairs.

CHAPTER 3

Grace made her way down to the breakfast room early the next morning, unable to sleep well after her encounter with Thomas. Making her way through the grand house, she thought about how nice it might have been to host such an event herself when she had been the Countess of Camden. It would not have been the same, however, as her husband's house in Yorkshire had never really felt like home in the six years she had lived there. With how out of place she had always felt, she would not have wished to entertain even if her husband and his late mother, the dowager countess, had permitted it.

Arriving at the breakfast room, Grace smiled as she found Moira, Countess of Geffen, directing footmen with loaded platters of breakfast fare toward the buffet. She was happy to see her friend looking so at ease playing hostess. Even with a large group about to descend on her house for the week, Moira appeared unruffled.

Grace made her way over to the buffet and poured herself a cup of coffee, as she would need something stronger than tea to sustain her this morning. She needed to catch up with Moira and share some uncomfortable truths that might shorten her stay at Geffen House. As much as she was dreading the conversation, she owed it to her friend to be truthful regarding why she was there, even though she should still be in full mourning. Looking Moira's direction, Grace caught her eye and felt both happy and guilty as Moira beamed at her in welcome.

Moira, who had always been beautiful with her masses of glossy, sable curls, looked even more resplendent than Grace remembered. Having grown into a woman and becoming a mother since Grace had seen her last, Moira now had soft, feminine curves. And she exuberated an uncontainable joy, almost seeming to glow, brightening every room she entered. Grace had desperately missed her in the eight years since they had last been together, the two having once been like sisters.

Grace first met Moira ten years before when they started at Lady Evelyn's finishing school. Their fathers wanted the best for their daughters, and that meant preparing them for what lay ahead in their future, mainly marriage. Being in the lower level of the aristocracy as a baron, Moira's father wished to provide his daughter with the best possible chance at a good match and hoped to elevate the family's place in society. In the case of Grace's father, he simply wanted her to be happy and hoped the school might fill the void of feminine guidance in her life. Thus, in the fall of 1809, both girls found themselves enrolled in a program to teach them the ways of the aristocracy and how to run a lord's household.

Lying in bed that first night at school, sheets pulled tight beneath her chin, Grace didn't know what to think or feel. At only fifteen, she felt extremely out of place being away from home for the first time. She was scared to leave her father, but as her mother had died when she was only five years old, she understood that he wanted her to have the education and influence that only a woman could provide, and Lady Evelyn was well regarded as the most genteel and elegant of ladies. Those who went through her school program were refined and well-spoken, even if soft and deferential in speaking, as they were taught to always defer to their betters. Along with those above their station, all men, regardless of title, were included in the category of "betters." Grace wished to become like Lady Evelyn herself and make her father proud. However, the desire to please did not make her any less terrified of what may be involved in preparing for her coming-out in the next few years.

Unable to sleep with these thoughts in her head, she heard a voice the next bed over ask if she was also afraid. From that moment on, Moira and Grace were inseparable.

The two young women were so attached to one another that, through countless letters over that first year, they pleaded with their fathers to allow Grace to stay with Moira's family for the first part of summer. This was where Grace met Thomas, Moira's younger brother. Grace found him to be a nice young man, two years her junior, and he set out on adventures with them over the summer. They had all gotten along well —which was why his behavior in the library had come as such a shock. Much had changed for them in the intervening years, and Grace had lost touch with Moira as her life had changed, but she did not expect to find things so drastically different. She was unsure how Moira would react if she learned about last night's encounter.

"Grace," Moira exclaimed, "I am so glad you were able to join us this week and agreed to come a day early so we might catch up a bit before everyone else arrives! It has been too many years since we've had a chance to properly catch up with one another. I am so glad I ran into you at Hatchard's last week." Warmth shining from her eyes, Moira gripped Grace's hands and looked happy to reconnect with her old friend. Grace returned her smile and clutched her hands just as firmly. Even amid her uncertainty about being here this week, the one thing Grace was sure about was how much she wished to reestablish their relationship.

"I'm grateful for the invitation, and I am so happy to see your sweet face again, but I must confess something to you," Grace said nervously. "Is there someplace we may talk?"

"Of course," Moira responded with a furrowed brow. "Give me a moment to finish setting up here and then we can take our drinks out to the veranda. It is such a lovely morning and already warming up."

"Thank you. I don't mean to impose, as I know you have much to organize, but it would really ease my mind if I could explain what has happened over the past several years. I really have missed you Moira," Grace said.

"And I you," Moira said with another smile. "Go on ahead and I'll be out shortly with some tea and pastries."

About fifteen minutes later, Moira joined Grace in the chairs out on the large stone balcony overlooking the estate's back garden.

"It really is beautiful here," Grace murmured, enamored by the view. She had been transfixed by watching hummingbirds and insects go about their work, flitting from one floret to the next, collecting the nectar that awaited them in the plants along the balcony. Enjoying the warmth that crept up the stone steps beside her as the sun rose for the day, she closed her eyes and tipped her head back, seeking peace before possibly ruining the morning with what she needed to share.

"Yes, summer in Kent really is one of the most extraordinary experiences," Moira said as she settled in beside Grace. "I love returning to Geffen House once the season is over, it is such a peaceful change to the bustle of London. While I do love all the entertainments of the city, after a while, I crave a slower pace.

There is nothing more wonderful than to be wrapped up in the clean country air and to enjoy time with my children." She had a dreamy look about her as she gazed over the green landscape in the direction of the marsh and the sea beyond it, barely visible in the distance.

Shaking her head to pull her back to the present, Moira's demeanor abruptly turned serious as she straightened her posture and turned to look at Grace. "Now, do talk to me. What has you so concerned? I know we have not seen each other in over seven years, since your father passed, but you know you will always be one of my truest friends. You can tell me anything." She was so sincere that it made Grace feel even more guilt for taking advantage of her hospitality.

"I'm sorry I was so distant," Grace said. "I did not want to lose touch with you for so many years. Keeping in contact became . . . difficult . . . after my marriage." Seeing nothing but love in Moira's expression, Grace built up the courage to continue. "I'm afraid I'm here under less-than-ideal circumstances, and I am hoping our past friendship will make you more amenable to forgive me for coming here under false pretenses," Grace admitted. "I do not wish to take advantage of your hospitality, and I won't stay if I do not have your blessing."

Moira, now looking even more concerned, leaned over and took Grace's hand. "When you say you are here under difficult circumstances, what do you mean? Are you in trouble?" she asked gently.

Grace looked down at the napkin in her lap as it was too difficult to look into Moira's kind eyes as she shared part of her story. "I'm not necessarily in trouble, but by the rules of polite society, I should not be here," she said, twisting the cloth between her fingers, still unable to make eye contact. "You are aware that my husband died recently, but the truth is he died only four months ago, and I should still be in full mourning. It's hardly proper for me to be at a social engagement for at least another two months, or even eight." Blushing deeply, she finally lifted her head to face Moira. "I should not have accepted your offer to join you here, it is most improper. If you wish me to go, I will. The last thing I want is for my indecent behavior to reflect poorly upon you." She could feel the strain on her body as she tensed in anticipation of Moira's reaction.

"Of course I want you here, and I will always forgive you," Moira said without hesitation, a reflection of both her good nature and how close they had once been. "But may I ask why you have chosen to be here instead of at home remembering your husband?"

"I'm rather at the mercy of my husband's family at the moment," Grace admitted with some embarrassment. "The new Earl of Camden was keen to return to the city and insisted I accompany him and his wife. Not wishing to miss any entertainments in London, he decided we would no longer adorn mourning once we reached the city."

"So you cannot honor your husband because it would reflect poorly on them if they did not continue to do so as well," Moira said, quickly grasping Grace's circumstances.

"I cannot upset them. I am reliant on their support," Grace said softly. "I am looking for a placement as a companion or governess so I may be able to leave them as soon as possible, but for now I am reliant on their hospitality." She once again looked down, unable to meet the curiosity in Moira's eye. She hurried to preempt the questions Moira would ask if given the opportunity. "When you asked me to join you here, I selfishly saw it as an opportunity to get away for a while as I try and find my next place. I can't be around them, but I will leave if you don't think it proper for me to be here," she said.

At this point, Grace was past decorum and willing to beg to find peace away from her husband's relatives. Practically vibrating from the stress she was under, she could feel a dull ache beginning in her temples and wished only to disappear. Grace was deeply ashamed that she had sunk so low as to take advantage of her friend in such a way. She couldn't bear imagining how her father would feel about her being in such a position.

"Oh, you poor dear," Moira said, rushing to envelope her in an embrace, and Grace had to keep herself from bursting into tears. "Of course you should stay. I don't care that you should still be in mourning, I care that you are happy and well. I am glad you are here," Moira said, squeezing her tightly. Relief flooded Grace, and she melted into the comfort of her friend's arms.

Pulling back, she wiped at her eyes and leaned her forehead against Moira's shoulder.

"Thank you," Grace said through a lump in her throat, her relief palpable. "I am so sorry to be an imposition, but I can't tell you what a weight you have lifted off my shoulders. I did not like feeling as if I were deceiving you, not knowing my full situation, and I am grateful you are still willing to have me." They embraced for a long moment, simply enjoying being with one another again.

Leaning back and wiping a stray tear of her own, Moira said, "Now, getting back to the business at hand, because you are not well-known in London society and the earl was not often out in the city or active in Parliament, we should be able to keep your mourning status relatively quiet. No one knows the details or timing of his passing, but should it become known, we can use the excuse that you are a dear friend and practically family to justify your presence here. Many accept that those in mourning can still attended family events."

"Thank you," Grace said sincerely. "I don't suppose you know of anyone looking for help? Would any of the guests coming be in need of a governess or companion?" She hated to ask but was desperate to find a placement as soon as possible.

"Is it really as dire as that?" Moira asked gently, trying not to pry. Grace appreciated Moira reigning in her curiosity as the renewed relationship between them was still fragile, no matter how deep their bond had once been.

"I'm afraid so. It is untenable to remain with the new earl, and I do not have the means to establish a home for myself." Humiliated, Grace left out how no one had cared about her well-being enough to ensure her a widow's portion when her marriage contract had been negotiated, forcing her to either rely on family support, which she did not possess, or find a means to establish her own way.

"I am happy to ask around once everyone arrives," Moira assured her. "Is there anyone in particular you wish me to inquire with?"

"No, not that I know of," Grace replied. "Who is on the guest list?" She was quite curious to find out who would be there other than Thomas and the Duke of Carrington.

"Well," Moira began, thinking through her guest list. "There will be twenty-four guests total in attendance. Nearly half will be composed of married couples, some elderly relations, and chaperones for some of the young ladies. But there will also be several eligible gentlemen." With a twinkle in her eye, Moira paused before asking, "Have you considered the possibility of finding a new husband? Some of my husband's friends will be here, and they are wonderful men. Mr. Sidney Bright, Captain Claybourn, and the Duke of Carrington are all eligible, and Fitz and I love them dearly." She was clearly keen on the idea of playing matchmaker.

"No. I will never marry again," Grace said firmly. "I would much rather be responsible for myself."

Moira's look of concern returned at her flat denial

of the idea of marriage. To many it would seem to be an ideal solution, but Grace saw it as stifling.

"We really do need to spend time catching up on the last few years. It sounds as if there is a much larger story here and that you truly are in need of an old friend," Moira said.

CHAPTER 4

The opening dinner of the house party had only just commenced, but Henry was already gritting his teeth. Moira sat him between a young lady, Jane, he thought someone had said, who had just finished her first season unattached, and Lady Wrexham, who had an available daughter accompanying her this week. Each was trying to ingratiate themselves to him, for a single duke of marriageable age was considered a top prize. Both seemed to want to win.

He shot a glare in Moira's direction as Lady Wrexham spoke ad nauseam about how her precious Anne could do no wrong and would be such a good influence on other young ladies if she held the position of duchess. Moira sent him a wry smile in return, as if to say, *Sorry, deal with it and be nice.* He could have happily killed her for putting him in this situation and convincing him to come in the first place. Reid, sitting across from him and catching the direction of the glare, smirked.

He turned toward Jane, the lesser of the two irritants, and tried to make conversation. "Is this your first time attending a house party?" he asked, not knowing how else to begin.

"Oh, yes. I'm having such a lovely time. It's wonderful to make such nice, new acquaintances, don't you think?" she simpered, coquettishly looking up at him while batting her eyelashes. Henry couldn't stand such affected and insincere comments, but he could hardly blame the poor young lady for behaving in such a manner. From what he recalled during his time at Cambridge, this was how young women in the *ton* were taught to act in order to catch a man, having been told their entire lives that making a good match was their greatest purpose. He hated that women's agency had been reduced to focus on such a goal.

As he half listened to her prattle on about how much she had enjoyed being out last season, he reflected on how unfortunate it was that most eligible ladies on the marriage market were so young. Listening to Jane, he couldn't imagine setting up a life with a young woman like her, half his age and with little comprehension of how to deal with the complications of life. How would such a young lady make a good partner for him and be able to handle all the responsibilities of a duchess? While he was nowhere near ready for a wife, he would like to be with someone older who had more life experience.

Glancing down the table, he noticed the woman from the library the evening before. Lady Harcourt was how Moira had introduced her to him. She seemed to be engaged in conversation with the gentleman sitting on her left, Mr. Stanhope, and Henry noticed Sidney sitting to her right, the lucky bastard. She turned her head, and Henry gazed at her in appreciation. He'd not had much of a chance to take in her appearance last night, consumed by ensuring her safety, but now had time to admire her surreptitiously.

She was not an overly tall woman, though she did not appear delicate. Her hair shone in the candlelight, making the deep honey-blonde color appear more of a tarnished gold. Her gaze was kind and attentive as she listened to Stanhope; and while he could not discern their color clearly due to the distance between them at the table, he recalled her eyes being a deep, soulful brown. The longer he looked at her, the more beautiful she became, until he was yanked back to the present by Lady Wrexham demanding his attention. "Apologies, my lady," he said, putting on his warmest smile. "I'm afraid I was drifting, a bit tired after the journey here," he said, not lying outright.

As the meal progressed, he found his glance returning to Lady Harcourt and he recalled what little he had learned of her from Fitz during breakfast.

"I don't really know much about her, why do you ask?" Fitz had inquired as he slathered homemade preserves thickly on his croissant.

"No reason really," Henry demurred, "I ran into her about the house last evening and I'm not familiar with her. I was just curious." He did not feel the need to share how he met the lady. Even though Henry trusted him implicitly, the near assault he walked in on included Fitz's brother-in-law, and it was not his business to share, as it could have negative implications for Lady Harcourt.

Pausing to reach for the teapot, Fitz looked thoughtful saying, "she's a bit of a mystery really. She and Moira were close friends when they attended a finishing school together in the years before their coming-out. I'd not had the chance to meet her, however, as her father died when they were eighteen. Her come-out was delayed, as she was in mourning, so I did not see her during the season when I met Moira, and she was unable to attend our wedding. After that, she rather seemed to disappear. She married the Earl of Camden after her mourning was concluded and disappeared to the North until she was widowed. Moira ran into her at a bookshop last week and was overjoyed to restart their acquaintance. Moira insisted she come this week and we had to scramble to find another gentleman to make up the numbers. I think she invited Stanhope to be a balance."

The fact that Moira was resuming a relationship explained why Lady Harcourt had been at the house earlier than most of the other guests. Henry supposed the two women wanted time to get reacquainted after so long. Their previous relationship also explained why Thomas intimated that they knew each other. The fact that she was a widow, and no one seemed to really know anything about her, was intriguing.

Dessert was set out at last, meaning dinner would finally be concluding. He forced a smile back onto his face as Jane exclaimed in delight about her adoration for whatever they were being served. It was going to be a very long week indeed.

Moira stood and announced that it was time for the ladies to retreat to the parlor for conversation while the men had their port. Grace breathed a sigh of relief.

Dinner was not unpleasant, but unused to spending time in social settings, Grace found it taxing. Moira had thoughtfully placed her between Mr. Bright and Mr. Stanhope, two amiable men who had been easy to converse with overall, thus easing much of her anxiety. She found Mr. Bright's name to suit him, as he had a lively and witty personality, but it was Mr. Stanhope who monopolized most of her attention throughout the evening, informing her about his keen interest in birds. He was quite the bird-watcher and was excited to be in Kent, where a variety of fowl he rarely saw made their home along the marshes of the areas coastal landscape.

Grace had been both flattered and overwhelmed by his attention. She just wished his interests were a little more exciting. But it had been easy enough to listen and nod or 'hmm' in agreement every once and awhile. Even though she had shut down Moira's suggestion of finding a new husband, she couldn't help but wonder if she were still playing matchmaker, as it did not escape Grace's notice that both men were unmarried. Now, though, she was happy to escape from such close quarters where conversation was expected. With the women, she could fade into the background as they gossiped with one another.

When the men rejoined them for the evening festivities—Moira had arranged for a renowned pianist to play for them—Grace noticed the duke when he entered the room. It was futile to linger on his presence, as he was far above her socially, but she was preoccupied thinking about him anyway. She worried that he would mention walking in on her with Thomas the night before. Even a hint of impropriety could hurt her chances of finding a good placement, which was why attending the house party so soon after her husband's passing was foolish. Adding in word of an encounter that may look like a compromising situation could prove ruinous.

While Carrington had acted in her defense, seeming to understand that Thomas's advances were unwanted, many in society would blame her for finding herself underdressed and alone with him in the first place. While she hoped an acquaintance of Moira's would not think that way, she couldn't be sure if he would say something that could harm her chance at securing a future for herself away from those who no longer wished to bother with her.

Even with her concerns, Grace admired how handsome he looked in his bottle-green coat and how broad it made his shoulders appear. Looking over, he caught her gazing at him. She turned away quickly, but not before noticing his repressed smile that brightened his gray eyes, making her blush.

Her attention was unpleasantly diverted, however,

when she saw Thomas staring at her as well. He was whispering with another young man, presumably his friend, and both appeared to have been enjoying liberal amounts of the wine from dinner. She feared they were discussing her, as the friend was sneering in her direction while Thomas was laughing. Her face now burning, she was almost certain Thomas was talking about what happened last night, exaggerating the details and her level of willingness, as young men are wont to do. Feeling sick to her stomach, she unthinkingly joined the applause as the pianist was introduced.

The music was beautiful, but Grace hardly took it in as she worried about Thomas. Would he spread untrue rumors about her that would paint her as a loose and immoral woman? She was a widow, so some behavior would be overlooked and forgiven more freely, but not if the behavior was seen as egregious. She already had plenty working against her and could not allow rumors to spread too. It's possible she was being paranoid, but she could not shake the thought and became more restless as the concert continued.

The only thing Grace could think of that might persuade Thomas to desist was his sister and the duke. And she certainly didn't want to inform Moira, who was already going out of her way to support her and who may not take kindly to the news regarding her brother. But Carrington displayed a profound influence on him yesterday. Maybe she could talk with the duke and ask him to speak to Thomas on her behalf. She would have to pray the man was as good as Moira believed.

CHAPTER 5

It was a beautiful day, but being the end of July, it was shaping up to be a scorcher. At just before noon, the sun was bright enough to make everyone seek the cover of shade. Henry squinted as he made his way to the garden, looking for Lady Harcourt. The grounds of Geffen House really were quite remarkable, and Henry loved exploring them whenever he came to visit. She had not specified where to meet within the garden, but he made his way toward the wisteria arch visible from the back of the house.

This morning he had been surprised to find a note from Lady Harcourt asking him to meet. She had written succinctly and with urgency:

Your Grace,

Please forgive my forward nature in writing you when we have barely been acquainted. I wish to thank you for coming to my rescue the other evening, and I must beg of you one more service to prevent irreparable harm in an already precarious situation. I ask you to meet me in the garden at noon.

Your grateful servant,
Lady Grace Harcourt, Dowager Countess of Camden

Henry noted how the writing became less refined at the end, and he did not wish for her to be in distress and would help if at all possible. He suspected the behavior he observed from Thomas last evening was what had prompted her to reach out to him. Henry had seen the young upstart laughing with his friend while gesturing toward Lady Harcourt, and he hoped he could ease her mind regarding his discretion. He was alarmed at the mention of this precarious situation. He was eager to see her.

As he approached the arch leading into the garden, Henry saw Lady Harcourt just inside, near a bench with her back facing him. He noticed the gentle curve of her neck, his eyes tracing it into her upswept hair that was now a burnished gold in the midday sun, contrasting with her creamy skin. His boots crunched on the gravel path as he entered the garden, and she started at the sound, quickly turning toward him.

"You startled me, Your Grace," she stuttered with wide eyes as her hand lifted to clutch her heart. His eyes naturally followed the motion of her hand and he admired the swell of her breast. Reprimanding himself, he looked up at her face and saw that she had dark shadows beneath her eyes.

"I apologize, my lady. I did not mean to sneak up on you," he said. "Are you well?" he asked, concerned by her pallid appearance.

"Yes, I am well," she replied. "And it is not your fault. I have always spooked easily and should have known better than to have my back turned." She seemed uneasy, but no harm was done.

"Shall we walk?" he asked. "I believe I heard that a luncheon was being planned near the stream, just south of here. Why don't we move in that direction?" Lady Harcourt nodded in acknowledgment, and they started further into the garden.

Henry stepped forward to walk beside her and had to restrain himself from taking her arm, though he longed to touch her. She still seemed skittish, and since he really did not know the lady, he did not feel the gesture would be appreciated, even if it was appropriate for a gentleman to offer. They walked on together, the silence awkward for a moment before she broke it.

"Thank you for meeting with me, Your Grace," she said softly. "I know this is most unusual as we have not really made each other's formal acquaintance and it was quite improper for me to contact you. I would beg your forgiveness for my boldness, I am usually never so forward, but I'm afraid I am quite desperate." She was visibly agitated and wringing her gloves in her hands. Not looking at him as she spoke, her eyes fixed on the footpath before them.

"My lady, please don't be anxious," he said, wanting desperately to set her at ease. "I can assure you that I am not a gossip and would never share the particulars of an event that was truly not of my own affairs." He paused and turned toward her, reaching out and placing his fingertips on her elbow to pause her. "You seem to be in great distress. Are you sure Thomas did not harm you the other evening?"

Stopping, she turned toward him and lifted her eyes to his. Her lips trembled and she took in a wobbly breath before responding, "I admit to being a bit shaken by the events of a few days ago, but I promise I am well." She tried to sound reassuring but was not entirely successful. "Thomas took me by surprise, but with your assistance, no lasting harm was done." She paused to gather herself and had a determined look when she turned to face him again. "I would like to ask you a favor, beyond the silence on the matter which you have so kindly offered. While I don't believe it would be in Thomas's best interest to talk widely about what transpired, I fear yesterday evening he may have been sharing misleading information with his friend regarding me. I know that he would do anything to maintain your good favor as a duke. Would you be willing to talk with him on my behalf and ensure that he will not spread what transpired any further?"

"Yes, I will speak with Thomas if that is what you desire," he agreed. "But, my lady, he is at fault entirely in this situation. I do not think he would wish to speak of it, as it would only reflect poorly upon him. You are blameless."

Looking anxious still, she explained, "I understand that, and so it seems do you, but others may not see it that way." She paused and he did not interrupt her. He waited for her to continue, as it seemed she was gathering her thoughts and trying explain what she meant. "If it were to become known that I was found alone with a man after hours, regardless of whether or not I desired his advances—which I can assure you I did not —many will say that I was asking for such attention by placing myself in such a situation." Henry hated it, but he knew how society operated and that there was truth in her words.

"As for whether Thomas would speak of it," she continued, "I don't know. But I do know how men like to discuss their supposed conquests with friends." Once again, Henry had to agree she had cause to be concerned. "I fear this is what I observed transpiring last night, which is what prompted me to ask for your assistance." She looked up at him with a hesitant yet hopeful expression. "I know Thomas has always sought to be held in high regard, and while I don't know if he was actually boasting in this manner, I know he would not speak of me again if you asked him not to."

Feeling chastened, Henry realized she was right. Most would not give the benefit of the doubt to a woman in such a situation, and it could in fact ruin her reputation. "I'm sorry to say you are correct in how many would view your situation," he told her. "I will have a word with Thomas for you," he said. "However, I don't normally like to use my title as a method of persuasion, as I have seen too many others abuse such influence." He saw her cringe under the weight of her request. "But," he continued, "I believe you are right that it will be used for the greater good here, and I will do what I can to protect you." Lady Harcourt bowed her head and whispered her thanks, but she still seemed to be wound tight.

"Is there any other way I may be of assistance?" he asked. "Pardon me for being so persistent, but it seems like you are still worried about something. I can assure you that you are safe with me, and I'll make sure no harm comes to your reputation if I can help it."

She caught her breath at his statement and slowly restarted down the path. "You are observant, Your Grace," she said after a moment. "I am rather tired after a sleepless night, and I am not entirely sure I should be here. I fear I may be taking advantage of an old friend's hospitality."

He was surprised but happy to find a companion who felt as uneasy as he did at the house party. Curious, he asked her, "How is it that you know the countess?" Of course, he had learned of their friendship from Fitz the day before, but he was eager to hear what Lady Harcourt had to say about the matter herself.

"We became friends in our teenage years when our fathers sent us to the same finishing school," she offered. "We were as close as sisters for a few years, but I'm afraid I lost touch with her once we left school, as my father died and then shortly after I was married."

"Fitz told me you are recently widowed, my lady. Might I know your late husband?" he asked.

She seemed to become more withdrawn at his question but still answered him. "My late husband was the Earl of Camden. I would be surprised if you knew him, as he did not often move in London society."

"I am sorry to hear you lost him. How long have you been out of mourning?" At his inquiry, she began to deeply blush. They had arrived at a beautiful, old elm tree, and she paused, placing her hand against the trunk as if the question left her in need of support. Taking a deep breath, as if she needed courage to answer the question, she slowly turned to face him so she could look him in the eyes.

"Truthfully, Your Grace, I should not yet be out of mourning." Henry was surprised by her response, but schooled his features so she would continue. "My husband passed only four months ago, so I should not be at this house party at all, but I find myself rather desperate to be away."

CHAPTER 6

Grace could hardly believe she had allowed herself to speak so boldly. Had she truly just shared her shame with an almost complete stranger? For some reason, she felt comfortable with him, like she could confess all her worries and he would take care of her. He had offered more than once to help her after all, and Moira had vouched for his character as a friend of Fitz's. But now, after her declaration, she feared he may not treat her with the same kind understanding. Yet as she gazed at him, she did not see disgust or condemnation on his face. Rather, he held a look of gentle concern with his mouth tipped down ever so slightly, accentuating his firm lips, and the skin around his eyes faintly crinkled.

"Is this the thing that has you feeling so desperate?" he asked, avoiding any trace of judgment in his tone. He waited patiently for her to respond, and she felt an overwhelming urge to open herself up and tell him everything, even more than she shared with Moira the previous morning.

Grace began to walk again, squinting against the sun, forcing him to keep pace. "I'm afraid I find myself needing a placement as a companion or governess . . ." she began hesitantly, "and I need to do so quickly." Saying it out loud so plainly was both a relief and a humbling reminder of what she needed to keep her focus on, rather than the man beside her who was proving a distraction with his very solid and manly presence.

"Lady Geffen and I reconnected a week ago after many years," Grace continued, refocusing on the matter at hand, "and when she invited me here, I saw an opportunity for a brief respite before I take up work. I decided to attend even though it is painful for me to abandon propriety regarding mourning, but I desperately needed a break from my husband's family while I plan for the future. I have made the countess aware of this, as I do not want to take advantage of her friendship," it was important to her that Carrington understood this. "She thinks she will be able to protect me from gossip or judgement if my circumstances are uncovered." Grace desperately hoped he would understand, and seeing him in silent contemplation, without comment or judgement, she felt emboldened to continue.

"Moira may be able to shape the narrative," Grace started, forgetting to retain formality in her address, "but I am still worried about how it may look to bend the rules in such a way when there are already dangers to my reputation that could impede my securing a placement."

"From where I stand and from what I have observed of you," Carrington said, "I don't see anything of concern. What has you in such a hurry to find employment?" he asked. There seemed to be an edge of disbelief that her circumstances were as dire as she had painted them. "Do you not have family that can support you? Or your late husband's family? Surely you must have something or someone you can fall back on while you take time to consider your future."

"No," Grace said, her cheeks flushed. "I must find work as soon as possible." As embarrassing as the situation was, she knew she would have to fully explain things for him to understand, weary as she felt at the prospect.

"I'm afraid there was no agreed-upon widow's portion when my marriage contract was drawn up, and I will need to support myself moving forward." She saw his disbelief at her neglect, but continued. "My father died when I was eighteen, only a few weeks shy of when I was set to make my come out to society. I missed the season, as I was in mourning. And as the only surviving child in my family, the title and estate were passed to my cousin, Edwin." She swallowed hard; it was difficult to recall that time. She loved her father dearly, and his passing left her without any immediate family and feeling desperately alone.

"My cousin allowed me to stay in our family home for that first year while I mourned and had nowhere else to go, but as soon as the period of mourning was over, he no longer wished to be responsible for me. Rather than allowing me to come out the next year and find a husband on my own terms, he quickly and quietly arranged for my marriage to Camden so he would not need to financially support a season." She heard Carrington give a derisive grunt.

Sensing the duke's agitation, she said truthfully, "Edwin was never cruel to me, but he also did not care for me. He simply saw me as a burden and no longer wanted to have any responsibility for me. It seems that lack of care extended to the marriage negotiations, and he did not take the time to look over the contract, meaning he did not ensure my welfare should I lose my husband."

Grace was now bright red and in utter disbelief over the secrets she revealed to this man. She had no idea what had come over her, not even sharing as much with Moira. It was mortifying to admit being an afterthought to those who should care for you. But there was something about the duke's kind eyes and the way he listened that made the words pour out. She felt drawn to him, intuitively sensing that she and her confidences were safe.

"That is simply unconscionable," Carrington said through gritted teeth. Genuinely angry on her behalf, Grace had watched his shoulders grow stiffer as she shared her story. She was touched by his obvious concern. "What about your husband's family, can they not keep you on in the family home?" he asked, trying to find a glimmer of hope.

Grace laughed, attempting to keep the bitter edge off her tone. "No, they wish to have nothing to do with me." Now squinting at the increasingly bright sun, she said, "The dowager countess, my mother-in-law, disliked me and poisoned much of the family against me. She passed as well, a few months before my husband did, but the damage had already been done." She grew quiet for a moment thinking about her life in Yorkshire, and Carrington allowed her the space. "As I did not provide an heir," she continued, "the earl's cousin, who was no fan of mine, inherited everything."

Grace was unsure just how honest to be with the duke, but considering all she revealed thus far, she decided there was nothing to lose. "The new earl's wife wants me out of the house. And the earl has become increasingly attentive to me in a way that I am not comfortable with, so I would like to move on as quickly as possible," she finished softly.

Now that Grace had let it all out, it felt like an emotional cleanse, and she exhaled with a full, shaky breath. However, the tension from recalling everything that had so drastically changed her circumstances over the past seven years made her head throb. She felt a sharp pain building behind her right eye from lack of sleep and from straining against the midday sunlight.

At her final admission that she may not be safe in her own home, the duke let out what almost sounded like a growl. "I am sorry to hear you have been treated so poorly," he said after taking a moment to tamp down the anger rippling across his face. "Is there no way your cousin will agree to support you again, even temporarily, as your husband's family will not?" he asked.

"I wrote to Edwin after my husband passed and

asked if I might return to my childhood home," Grace answered. "He responded that he was now married and that having me in the house would make his wife uncomfortable, that she would feel as if I were trying to assume her place in the home. He told me that it was now my in-laws' place to take care of me, as I had married into their family. He no longer felt it was his responsibility to support me," she said with downcast eyes, hurt remembering how her cousin had abandoned her.

"The truth is," she said, feeling utterly defeated, "I have no place to go unless I can procure a position somewhere. That's why it is so important for me to keep my reputation intact, so I might find a place more easily, and it's why I have asked for your help with Thomas."

She stumbled on the gravel pathway as a sharp pain lanced across her temple. Reaching out, she grabbed the duke's arm for support.

"Are you alright?" he asked, grasping her arm. She briefly leaned toward him while righting herself and caught a whiff of a clean, bright scent. He smelled heavenly, and she felt a bit light-headed. Whether the sensation was from the megrim she feared she was developing or just his proximity, she could not say.

"Yes, I think the sun just may be getting to me a bit," Grace deflected. "I really did not sleep well last night, anxious as I was. I promise I am fine. The fresh air is good for me," she said, trying to sound reassuring. "Let's keep walking toward the luncheon."

The turn of his lips told her Carrington did not

fully believe her, but he started walking again anyway, still supporting her arm. "So, to sum up your situation," he said, "if I understand everything correctly, you are here in less-than-ideal circumstances because you feel it may be worth the risk to escape your relations and secure a position."

As they exited the formal garden, Grace's head began to feel slow when she moved it, like it was filled with sand. She tried to concentrate on their surroundings to maintain her focus so she could respond to what he was saying, but was distracted by the place where his hand was supporting her and she felt tingly and warm.

"I understand your desire to secure something quickly, but why not wait to finish the proper length of mourning and thus lower your risk?" Carrington asked.

"I understand why you might feel that way," she said slowly, trying to keep a grasp on the thread of the conversation, her head feeling heavier by the minute, "but I'm not sure I can survive in my current situation with Camden that long." He went quiet as the gravity of her statement settled in.

Grace sighed, weariness washing over her. "I am not well-known in polite society, as I never officially made my come-out, and once married I spent all my time in Yorkshire. My good reputation is all I have to recommend me. With my abbreviated mourning period, the potential blow to my reputation is deeply concerning to me," Grace explained. "With nothing else to know about me, the *ton* will surely not be able to overlook my supposed sins should Thomas continue to boast."

Spilling her deepest fears so freely made Grace want to cry. She was trying valiantly to maintain her dignity in front of the duke, but feared she may not succeed. She was afraid now that he could see just how low she had fallen, he would never look at her with anything other than pity, and possibly contempt, again.

Swallowing her fear, Grace tilted her head up to look directly into Carrington's eyes. The movement emphasized the growing tension in her neck that pulled down into her shoulders, and her head throbbed as the bright sunlight lit him from behind, making him glow like a heavenly messenger. *Lord, he truly was handsome* Grace thought before the world around her began to swim.

CHAPTER 7

Henry grabbed hold of Lady Harcourt as she started to sway, gathering her against his chest. His heart pounded as he readjusted her in his arms so he wouldn't drop her. "Lady Harcourt? Can you hear me, are you hurt anywhere?" he asked as calmly as he could, trying not to panic. Her eyes fluttered open a moment later.

"I'm so sorry," she murmured with her head tucked against his chest. "A headache's come over me quite quickly, and I fear it now has me firmly in its grip." She clutched the fabric of his coat, bunching it in her fists to keep herself upright. He quickly maneuvered Lady Harcourt to his side so he could assist her in walking. They were almost at a large, old oak tree that stood only a few yards away. Henry guided her to the base of the tree and gently assisted her down so she could rest in the shade. Crouching to take stock of the situation, he was alarmed to see her face had turned as white as freshly laundered linens.

"What do you need?" he asked, keeping his voice low to not cause further distress. "Should I take you back to the main house?"

"No," she replied with closed eyes and a pinched brow. He noticed how beautiful she was even while obviously in pain. Briefly opening her eyes, she explained, "I believe the stress of everything compounded with little sleep and the bright, hot sun has simply overtaxed me." Closing her eyes again, she continued after a moment, "I just need to rest here for a few minutes, and then I will make my way to my room to rest more fully. Please make my excuses to Moira when you see her at the luncheon," she finished, still striving for politeness in her suffering.

"I will not leave you," he practically growled out, feeling protective and having no desire to leave her in anyone else's care. Just then, he noticed a footman ambling down a nearby path toward the stream, his arms were full of items that were undoubtably intended for the luncheon. "You there," Carrington called out toward the servant, "come over here, we need help." The footman jumped at the unexpected summons but quickly responded to Henry's commanding tone, making his way over to where they were huddled beneath the oak.

"How may I be of service, my lord?" the young man asked, rounding the tree. "Is she ill?" he asked upon seeing Lady Harcourt propped against the trunk. His eyes bulged in surprise.

"I need you to run down to where the luncheon is being set up and bring me back something cold to drink as well as some strong tea," Henry snapped, as if he were back in the army issuing commands. "Something bland and easy to eat as well—and be quick about it."

Lady Harcourt seemed to blanch when he mentioned food. Reopening her eyes and looking at the footman, she said, "Please, no food. Just the thought makes me feel nauseated and I don't think I could handle the scent," she said with a shudder. "But the tea and some cool water would be greatly appreciated." She attempted a wan smile, then leaned her head back against the bark and placed a hand over her closed eyes to block the sunlight.

"Of course. I will be back straightaway my lady," the footman said with a bow before scrambling off to secure the requested items.

Still crouching, Henry shifted to sit beside her on the ground. She unconsciously moved toward him, and he could feel the warmth of her arm radiating through his sleeve as she leaned into his side for support.

"I am so sorry, Your Grace," she said quietly. "I am absolutely mortified." Swallowing quite forcefully, as if trying to keep both tears and emotions back, she tried to thank him. "You have been so kind to me. First rescuing me the other night, and then assisting me today. It's my own fault I'm ill, what with my own fears and bad decisions," she said with a weak voice. "I am absolutely mortified that you should see me in such a state . . . and have had to listen to my misfortunes as well. I really am trying to take care of myself, but somehow, I have unburdened all of my problems onto you and made myself a nuisance."

"You have done no such thing," he responded immediately. "I asked how I might be able to help you, and I'm honored that you trusted me with your confidences." He really was flattered that she had chosen to place such trust in him. He had the feeling as she was sharing her background with him that it was not something she spoke of often. He genuinely wanted to find a way to make things just a bit easier for her, and talking with Thomas was an easy place to begin, though it did not feel like nearly enough, given her reduced circumstances and lack of familial support.

Looking at her as she leaned against him, he felt a warmth start in his chest and wanted to reassure her that she was not alone. "I am only sorry that the world has treated you so ill," he said softly, "you do not deserve it. If I can help in any way, I will." He paused before adding, "Please know that I will never share anything you have told me today. I'm glad you felt you could tell me, and I will honor your trust." His heart ached when she rested her head against his shoulder. Even with visible strain marring her features, she was beauty personified.

"Thank you," she said with a sigh.

The moment was broken when Henry heard a commotion from behind, the footman reappearing with a basket of items and a frantic Moira.

"Oh, Grace!" Moira exclaimed, rushing forward in a swirl of skirt and petticoats to crouch beside her. "Are you all right my dear?" she inquired, concern lacing her voice. "Hudson said you had been taken ill." *Grace,* Carrington thought. He had seen her name before on the note she sent, but hearing it for the first time, the name suited her.

"I'm alright," Grace reassured her friend. "It's just my head, as I have overtaxed myself."

"You dear, sweet thing. You are still suffering from megrims then?" Moira asked before looking over at Henry. Shaking her head, she said, "Grace is the only lady I've ever met who has no need to feign megrims as an excuse. Sadly, hers are painfully real."

Turning her attention back toward Grace, Moira grabbed the basket from the footman and began to procure bottles containing tea and water. Taking a glass of the water with a shaky hand, Lady Harcourt raised it to her lips and took a long draught. Henry was distracted thinking how full and pink her lips looked, even with her complexion still drawn with illness. He scowled, disgusted with his thoughts in this moment while the object of them was in a vulnerable position.

The footman handed Grace a napkin, as some of the water made its way down the front of her dress due to her unsteady hand. Looking up, she smiled and said, "It's Hudson, is it not? I remember you assisted me with my luggage when I arrived. Thank you for once again taking care of me."

With a goofy smile, he replied, "It's my pleasure, my lady. It is my job to make sure you are comfortable, and I am happy to do so." Watching in amusement, Henry believed Grace's kindness had endeared her to the footman for life, and he would not be surprised if

Hudson were a bit in love with her. Henry was sure the servant would be a shadow attending to her every need through the remainder of their time at Geffen House. Not that he could blame the young attendant, it was easy to fall under her spell.

"What else do you need, Grace?" Moira asked. "Do you need to rest? We can walk you back to the house and I'll get one of the maids to sit with you and find some headache powders."

Grace took another drink before passing the glass back to Hudson. "Yes, I think rest in a dark room is the only thing that will fix me at this point. Can you help me up?"

Before anyone else could claim the pleasure, Henry swiftly stood and offered his arm to her. When she grasped his hand, he felt a shock where their skin came into contact. Neither of them were wearing gloves due to the heat, and her skin was soft and warm. As Henry pulled her to her feet, she stumbled toward him with the force of her ascent, so he cupped her other elbow to steady her as she lifted her hand to cradle her aching head. Closing her eyes, she gently leaned forward and rested her forehead against his chest, as if the effort to hold it up herself was too much.

"Please forgive me, Your Grace," she said into his chest. "I fear the movement has caused my head to pound rather violently again. I need just a moment to resettle."

Moira came over, placed her hand on Grace's back, and moved it in slow, comforting circles. "Take all the time you need, dear. We will walk you up when you are ready," she said quietly, so as not to further disturb her. After a few deep and steadying breaths, Grace lifted her head, pulling back from Henry, and he immediately missed the weight of her against him.

"May I take your arm?" she asked him, seeking support. Henry offered it to her without comment, and they began a slow trek across the lawn back toward the house. The second they left the shade of the oak, she uttered a gasp of pain and quickly raised her hand to shade her eyes, before tucking her face into Henry's side, protecting her face from the glare. Without thinking, he swept her up into his arms and carried her to the house. Striding forward as quickly as he dared, he did not want to move too fast and jostle her. He thrilled at the feeling of her burying her face in the crook of his neck. All he could think about in the few minutes he had held her was how comfortable it was, how perfectly she fit in his arms, and how it felt like she had always been meant to be in them.

CHAPTER 8

"I hear you had quite the heroic moment earlier, Carrington. My maids were practically swooning with talk of the handsome duke who had rescued the damsel in distress and cradled her tenderly in his arms," Fitz teased.

Sending a stony glare Fitz's way while his other friends laughed, Henry grabbed a whiskey from the side table and sat down in an armchair with a large sigh. The men had just escaped the dance Moira had organized for the house party guests. He knew their departure would leave a shortage of gentleman for the ladies to partner with, and while he hated to upset Moira, Henry couldn't pass up the chance for a bit of peace, so he snuck off to Fitz's study with his friends in tow.

"Come now, Henry. We're only having a little fun," Reid said, reaching over and smacking him on the shoulder. "What really did happen?" he asked, his expression turned serious. "Is the lady well?"

"What I'm most interested in," Fitz interjected with a twinkle in his eye, "is what you were doing walking alone with the very lady you were inquiring about just yesterday."

"Oh, really?" Sidney piped up with a mischievous tone, leaning forward eagerly. "Do tell!"

Exasperated, Henry sighed in defeat. As much as he loved his friends, he knew they would not leave him alone unless he offered at least a few details. "It's nothing, really. I ran into her the other night and she was upset. Not knowing who she was, I asked Fitz about her at breakfast before you two yahoos arrived," he said, looking at Reid and Sidney. "She asked if she could talk with me today regarding a favor, and as we walked, the sun got to her and she developed a megrim. End of story."

"No, not the end of the story," Fitz replied. "You did not mention that she was upset when you saw her before. What's going on?"

"It is not my place to share," Henry responded firmly. "All you need to know is that she is a gentle and strong woman who has been dealt a raw deal in life, and I would very much like to help her if I can." His tone brokered no argument, and he hoped to firmly shut down his friends' line of inquiry.

"Fine," Sidney grumbled, taking his hint. "We'll leave you alone for now, but don't think this is the end of this topic."

"I wouldn't dream of it," said Henry, exasperated.

"Well, if nothing else, it did get you out of the luncheon," Reid offered. "I must say, there were a few disappointed mamas lying in wait to foist their unmarried daughters at the new and available duke." Reid's tone was teasing, but Henry knew there was truth in his statement.

Groaning, he slumped down in his chair as his friends had the nerve to laugh at him. Avoiding said mothers and daughters had been one of the main reasons for absconding from the group now. Slinging back the rest of his drink, he sat up abruptly and looked at Reid. "Honestly, how have you put up with it all these years? It's only been a few weeks since I've been out of mourning and I can't get away from them. Every time I'm in a social situation I have to watch my back so a scheming social climber will not entrap me, and I find myself in a situation where I would be forced to marry the girl." Grumbling, Henry added, "And I swear, the mothers are worse than the daughters." His friends laughed at the sentiment.

"I feel your pain, my friend. I really do." Reid stood and wandered toward the sidebar to pour himself another drink, the topic requiring it. Henry keenly understood his reaction and fought the impulse to do the same.

"I've learned to be cautious," Reid offered, "but things have gotten easier over the years. I've resisted marriage for so long that many of the mothers have lost their steam and now leave me alone. You are still too new and shiny, I'm afraid . . . and a duke is the ultimate prize. I'm still the heir apparent and will be only an earl when all's said and done." Chuckling, he raised his glass toward Henry in a salute.

"My god, I'm glad I'm a second son," Sidney offered. "While I still have those trying to make an honest man of me and force a match from one of my many conquests, there is not nearly the pressure the two of you face." The last was said with a visible shudder. "For now, I can continue to enjoy myself."

"It's just so damnably infuriating," Henry spat. "I never asked for any of this. I wasn't supposed to be the duke. I'm not prepared." Clutching his hair in his hands, he felt the tension in his shoulders crank up a notch thinking about all that came with his title. "I have so many people who are now relying upon *me* for their livelihood, and I have no idea the best way to manage land or an estate. I don't want to let anyone down . . . and my aunt will kill me if I harm the reputation of the family." Having finished his tirade, he sank into the armchair, imagining what it would feel like to disappear and leave all his responsibilities behind.

"Hey, come now. It's not all that bad." Fitz leaned forward and placed a comforting hand on Henry's knee. "I've been the earl for five years now, and I can help you learn what you need to know to manage the estate. I know you hate to do anything you don't think you're perfect at, but you're learning. And the good news is that unlike many of your peers, you are actually in the black and have the funds to do things properly. Reid and Sidney will get you up to date with what is happening in Parliament before the next session begins. As for marriage, it's not the death knell you all seem to think it is."

At Henry's exasperated look, Fitz raised his hands

in a placating manner. "Alright, I acknowledge that no one wants to be trapped into holy matrimony, it would definitely be better if the bride were of your own choosing. But truly, I cannot imagine my life without Moira in it," Fitz said with a dreamy look on his face. "She and our dear little ones have made my life immeasurably sweeter, and I only want the same for all of you." The last was said earnestly, and Henry couldn't help but acknowledge that maybe it would be nice to have a lovely woman by his side.

Reid laughed heartly. Coming to stand behind Fitz, he clapped a hand down on his shoulder. "I'm happy for you, truly I am. You know how much we all love Moira, and if I could find someone as sweet as her, I might be tempted to walk down the aisle myself. But you, my friend, have snatched up the only truly good woman." Reid's face turned dark as he then said, "With my odious father, I'll not be subjecting any woman, even if I despised her, to the firestorm that is my family. And I refuse to give my father the satisfaction of knowing his line is secure."

"It's true you are not in the best position at the moment," Fitz conceded to Reid, speaking carefully so as not to feed the dark cloud that now hung above the man's head. "But Henry," he said, turning toward him, "as much as you are currently resistant to the idea based on some overly pushy mothers, a duchess may be just what you need. Having someone to help support you as you bring your house into order is not the worst idea. Wouldn't it be nice to have someone by your side to help you, and arms to hold you at the end of a long day?"

Henry could concede that Fitz had a point. He had been waiting to pursue a wife until things with his estates were more settled and he felt comfortable in the role of duke, but maybe it would be easier to adjust to his new role if he had the support of a good woman by his side. He pondered the idea while his friends continued to natter on in the background, and the more he thought about it, the more he didn't hate the idea. If he could find a wife quickly, he could avoid the worst of the mamas who wished to climb the social ladder and would be all over him once the next season began. The image of Lady Harcourt came to mind as he thought about possibilities, and he shook his head to clear it, returning to the conversation of his friends.

CHAPTER 9

Grace awakened the next morning feeling much better, having rested thoroughly for the first time in days. While she still felt rather fragile, she could tell that the worst of the megrim was over. Snuggling back into her warm blankets, she did not yet wish to get up, preferring to stay cocooned for a bit longer. She was not ready to face reality, and judging from the lack of light peeping around the curtains, it was still rather early in the morning.

Yesterday was somewhat of a blur, but she was painfully aware that she had, for all intents and purposes, practically split open a vein as she spilled all her secrets to Carrington. What she remembered most was not so much her mortification, but his kindness toward her. He truly listened to her in a way that no one other than Moira had for the past seven years. He also seemed genuinely upset on her behalf, indignant at how both her blood relatives and in-laws had treated her.

She reflected on how drastically her life had changed once her father died. Losing her mother so young and not having siblings; he was everything to her. She had been so naïve leaving Lady Evelyn's school. Eagerly awaiting her come-out, she was comforted by the fact that her father was not putting pressure on her to marry immediately in her first season if she did not find a good match. He told her happiness in marriage, as his own had been, was more important than standing, title, or wealth. She had been looking forward to making her debut and having an enjoyable time at the balls and other events of the season with Moira.

When her father passed suddenly from what the doctors called *apoplexy*, two weeks prior to the opening of the season, her happiness and youthful ignorance were shattered. She had been thrust into mourning, and it was apparent that her coming-out to society would need to be postponed to the following season. Her cousin, Edwin, had quickly moved into the house, merely tolerating her as he took over the estate. She shouldn't have been surprised when he quietly arranged for her to marry one of his friends, Lord Camden, but it still came as a shock. It was an easy match in his mind, as his friend had been in need of a wife and was not picky, just looking to go about getting an heir. Having plenty of money already, Camden was not overly concerned with a large dowry, and Edwin could pawn her off for a reasonable price without putting a strain on his new coffers.

Everything had been decided without Grace's

knowledge, until she had been called to Edwin's study on the one-year anniversary of her father's death. He had informed her that, as her mourning period was now officially over, she would marry the Earl of Camden the very next day.

Camden had not cared for her one whit and seemed to only see her as a means to an end. She may as well have been a broodmare. After the marriage ceremony, there was no celebratory breakfast—he simply put her in his carriage, and they made their way north to his country seat in Yorkshire.

The next six years proved to be a test of Grace's strength. She had no friends around to keep her company, and the staff would not get to know her, as they were scared to lose their place should they be too informal with her. The worst part was her new mother-in-law, the dowager countess, who had taken an instant disliking to Grace and saw her as an inter-loper in her domain. The dowager ruled the household with a steely demeanor and refused to relinquish any control. Camden seemed content to allow his mother's reign of terror, so Grace had no role, authority, or purpose in her new home.

Grace had nothing to occupy her time, but her husband frowned upon many of her interests when she attempted to fill her time. He did not want her in the library, as he thought women should not be too educated, believing it led to discontentment. He did not like when she went to visit the tenants because, as a countess, she should not mingle with those below her own station. He also believed tenants should not become used to seeing their landlords too often, or they would start to take advantage of their generosity. And she was not permitted to work in the garden, though she loved plants and flowers, because he saw it as common and lowering.

For six years—until her husband met his untimely and violent end—she simply sat in the cold estate and withered away out of sheer boredom and loneliness. No one had ever been outright cruel to her; they simply ignored her, leaving her to molder away. It was as if the time spent there had made her forget who she was.

But now, back here in the South of England with her old friend, she could start to breathe again. Even with all the stresses she still had while working to secure her future, she felt a little more hopeful knowing that she had Moira on her side. It had been such an unexpected blessing to run into her at Hatchard's. She had only been in London for two days when she ventured out of the house to find a book-shop, planning to indulge her love of reading for the first time in years. Seeing Moira there, the two women had embraced with tears after instantly recognizing one another, even with the changes the intervening years had wrought upon them. It felt wonderful to have a loved one beside her once again.

And now, possibly, the Duke of Carrington could be counted as a friend as well. It was still much too early in their acquaintance to say if he could be a friend with any kind of certainty, but he had been so supportive of her yesterday and had not hesitated to defend her against Thomas. She believed his offer to help had been genuine, not simply a hollow, polite gesture expected of a gentleman. Then, when she had been foolish enough to press her body to its breaking point with her megrim, he had been right there to assist her.

Grace had been in too much pain to truly appreciate his attentiveness, but she could not forget how wonderful it had felt when he picked her up and carried her in his arms. Blushing, she burrowed further into the covers as she remembered how instantly safe and protected she had felt with her face nestled into the crook of his neck, his skin soft and warm. While she had been desperately trying to keep the harsh sunlight out of her eyes, she had not been above exploiting the situation either. He smelled delicious, like fresh laundry folded with lavender and citrus, and his chest was firm and strong. She shivered at the memory of it.

It had been a relief when they entered the house and exited the bright sunlight, but Grace had known she only had a moment longer in his arms. Servants had rushed forward to assist almost immediately, but she was glad when the duke sent them away and carried her upstairs himself, giving her another moment in his arms before he gently placed her on the bed. The cool, dark room and soft pillows under her aching head had been a relief to be sure, but she would have rather stayed cozied up with the duke if given a choice.

Allowing herself one last minute to revel in the memory, she thought about how handsome Carrington was. She had a weakness for darker coloring, and his eyes were such an expressive and stormy dark gray. Sighing, Grace shook the image out of her mind and forced herself to sit up and start the day.

Not wishing to call a maid for assistance so early, Grace went about washing and dressing herself. She put on a simple day dress in deep navy before sweeping her hair up into a twist. Even though she was breaking mourning by attending the party and abandoning black attire, her dark dress should help her avoid suspicion. And while she did not love her late husband, she still wanted to be respectful, finally having a better understanding of him in his death. This did not prove to be difficult, as much of her wardrobe was made up of serviceable gowns of strong fabric in deep colors that would not show stains or wear. The dowager had controlled the purse strings tightly and made sure Grace only had clothing that was practical in every sense. Sighing at her rather dowdy reflection, Grace made her way downstairs.

CHAPTER 10

Henry had woken early, having spent the night tossing and turning from the unceasing thoughts of marriage and Lady Harcourt. And rather than stay in bed, he went for a morning ride to clear his mind. The air was bracing and refreshing this early in the day, before any summer heat intruded. As his mount cantered along the trail, and reinvigorated by the breeze, Henry decided that he would use the next few days to learn more about Grace.

From what Grace had shared, Henry believed she possessed a strength unbeknownst to her to endure so much change and neglect since losing the protection of her father. Having been raised among polite society, she would have an understanding of the world he was now thrust into as an elite member of the peerage. The more he dwelled on it, the more he thought she could be an excellent prospect for his duchess. Returning to the stable, he took one last deep breath of the crisp morning air before dismounting the horse and handing her over to the groom for a good brushing down.

"She was good to me this morning, willing to ride even as I made her work hard so early. Be sure to give her an extra treat for her efforts," he told the groom as he affectionately petted the mare's nose. Smiling, the groom assured him he would take good care of her and treat her like a queen.

Taking off his riding gloves, Henry strode across the lawn toward the house. He hoped breakfast was ready, as he was hungry after his ride. While he enjoyed starting his day with some exercise, it usually left him famished. He was brought short on his mission, however, when he saw a gentleman stumbling toward the side door of the house, obviously returning to the estate after a night of drinking and carousing. As he strode closer, he recognized Moira's brother, Thomas, the very troublemaker he needed to talk to.

"I need a word with you," Henry growled while clenching Thomas's collar, preventing him from moving into the kitchen.

"What do you want?" Thomas sneered, once again not realizing he was addressing a duke. Disgusted by the gin fumes wafting off him, Henry let him go abruptly. Stumbling around at the unexpected release, Thomas recognized him. Immediately attempting a bow, he tripped over his own feet in his inebriated state. "Forgive me, Your Grace, I did not know it was you. What can I do for you?" His attempt at saving face was cloying and further irritated Henry.

"You need to clean up your act or you will only land

yourself in more trouble," he sternly admonished the younger man. "I sincerely hope you were not preying upon any other unsuspecting and unwilling young women last night." At this, Thomas's appeasing manner faltered.

Henry wanted to ensure his message regarding Grace came across loud and clear, so he grabbed Thomas's arms and looked him dead in the eye before proceeding. "I want your word that you will not speak to anyone about what you did to Lady Harcourt the other night. I will not have her good name smeared by the likes of you."

Obviously taken aback by the level of vitriol in Henry's delivery, Thomas dropped his smarmy smile.

"Because you are Moira's brother and I have nothing but love and respect for her, I am willing to give you the benefit of the doubt that you will conduct yourself as a gentleman, and we can discuss this issue no further," Henry said. "If, however, I hear from anyone, anywhere—even ten years from now—that you have hurt Lady Harcourt's reputation by bragging of a conquest to your friends, I will make you regret it. Are we clear?" he snapped.

Attempting to laugh off the situation, Thomas said, "Your Grace, it was only a little bit of innocent entertainment between two old friends, surely you cannot begrudge a man for taking advantage and having a little fu—"

He was abruptly cut off by Henry placing his arm across his throat, slamming him against the kitchen door.

"The Lady did not want your advances and you had no right to take any liberties without her express permission. She clearly told you no," Henry seethed. "Even if a lady were to give you permission in a similar situation, as a gentleman, you should give thought to their reputation before deciding to act." When Thomas opened his mouth to reply, Henry cut him off. "I would think long and hard about what you say next." He applied more pressure to make his point while being careful not to cut off Thomas's air supply.

Thomas held up his hands in surrender, and Henry eased away. Realizing he was beaten, Thomas grudgingly said, "I promise I will not mention the incident to anyone. No one needs to know, and I will protect her reputation."

"Good, now go and sleep it off," Henry barked as he walked away, releasing Thomas and leaving him doubled over to catch his breath.

Henry was fuming. Thomas's blasé attitude toward how he had treated Grace reaffirmed everything she had been afraid of yesterday when she asked him to speak to Thomas on her behalf. He was angry with himself for not initially seeing the seriousness of the situation or understanding why Grace had been so concerned.

Stomping off to find breakfast and cool his temper, he decided to find the lady afterward and let her know Thomas would no longer be a problem.

Later that morning, much less agitated after a delicious morning meal, Henry went to the library at Moira's direction to speak with Lady Harcourt. Opening the doors to the room, he found Moira's intuition had been correct. He discovered the lady in question sitting in a window seat, engrossed in a slender volume resting on her lap.

She hadn't noticed him yet, so Henry took the moment to observe her. She was still a little pale, and the shadows under her eyes hinted at the continued need for sleep, but overall, she appeared to be in much better condition this morning. Though nothing about her appearance was ornate—she was dressed in a muted navy and her hair was styled in an unfussy manner—she was still dazzling. Sitting in the window, the morning sun shone on her bent head, lending her golden hair and skin a glow that made her remaining pallor almost unnoticeable. She was clearly enjoying whatever she was reading, and a corner of her mouth perked up in a half smile while he watched.

As she flipped a page, he could see the dust rise from the noticeably old book and dance in a sunbeam that cut across the room. Her nose scrunched adorably, fighting the tickle from the swirling dust, and Henry felt his heart clench at the action; it was so unguarded and pure. A moment later, she let out a tremendous sneeze that seemed much too large for her diminutive frame. A laugh escaped him before he could contain it and Grace startled as she became aware of his presence.

Blushing deeply, she hung her head as if she were

ashamed to be caught in such a position. She hurried to scramble down from the windowsill and snapped the book shut, holding it behind her back.

"I'm sorry, my lady, please forgive me. I didn't mean to startle you. Please don't get up on my account, I just wanted to see if you were well this morning."

"I am quite well. Thank you, Your Grace," she answered while looking at the floor, cheeks aflame. "I'm afraid you caught me in a guilty pleasure." She quickly placed the book down, as if it were dangerous and she should not have possession of it.

"Why is reading something you should feel guilty about?" he asked, genuinely curious.

She blushed even deeper, a reaction he found charming, the color spreading down her neck to her chest. "I guess I'm still getting used to reading whenever I feel like it. It was not a pastime my husband or his family approved of," she said quietly, still staring at the floorboards.

Henry was astounded. "Well, I'm sorry for that," he said after a moment, unsure how to respond to such an indignity. From what Moira had implied earlier, reading had been a source of joy for her all her life. "You seem better this morning—were you able to rest?" he asked, returning the conversation to her well-being. "I was quite worried for you yesterday. You seemed to be in a great deal of pain." She finally looked up at him and smiled. He was once again struck by her beauty, even more so when she let out a genuine smile.

"I assure you I am well, Your Grace. I will need to take it slow today, but overall, I feel back to normal."

She looked down again. "I cannot thank you enough for your aid yesterday," she continued. "I must admit to being embarrassed by the desperate display I presented . . . It was bad enough that I was skirting the rules of decorum by meeting with you—and then to ask for your help as well. It's quite another thing to then fall ill and require further assistance." She began wringing her hands, distressed at the idea that she may have put him out.

He grabbed her hands to still them, wanting to put her at ease. He felt her slightly shudder at the contact, but she did not pull away. "Please, think nothing of it. I was not in the least offended, and I can assure you that I was happy I could be of assistance," he said, smiling down at her.

Grace returned a small smile, barely perceptible at the corners of her mouth, and he was once again transfixed by the plump shape of her lips. "The megrim has released its hold after a long night of needed sleep. And I was able to get some fresh air this morning, which is the best medicine." Henry was surprised to hear her echoing what he had thought himself on his morning ride.

"Good, I am glad to hear it," Henry said, before releasing her hands. "I also wanted to let you know that I spoke with Thomas this morning. He should not bother you again, and I believe he will think twice before saying anything about you in company." His brow furrowed just thinking about the miserable excuse for a man. The fact that he was Moira's brother was the only thing keeping him from giving Thomas a taste of what he really deserved, but for his friend he would keep himself in check.

"Thank you," Grace said. "I am sorry I asked you to use your influence in such a way, but I greatly appreciate that it hopefully had the intended effect."

"If it's what it took to get him in line, I was more than happy to throw my title around. I never asked for or wanted it, but I'm happy I've been able to use it for good," he told her.

She was puzzled by his cryptic statement, but instead said, "I sincerely appreciate your efforts. I cannot repay you. Hopefully the incident can be laid to rest, and there will be no more danger to finding a good position."

Henry hated the idea of her needing to work to support herself and felt anger rising within him. Recalling Fitz's comments about marriage from the day before, he realized that if he were to make her his wife, she would no longer need to worry about her future. The fact that he could help her as she supported him made Henry excited. He would need to think on the idea and use the next few days to learn more about her and see if they could have a life together.

"I'll take no more of your time," he informed her, getting ready to take his leave so he could ponder his own next steps. "I hope you will enjoy your book and not feel a shred of guilt about it."

The image of her delighted face and warm smile at his pronouncement stayed with Henry for the rest of the day.

CHAPTER 11

Afternoon tea left Grace feeling uneasy and overwhelmed, as the gossip swirled around her in the drawing room, the women chatting while the men were out on a ride around the estate grounds.

She had managed to keep mostly to herself in the library this morning as she continued recovering. The only one to disturb her had been Carrington, and she felt her cheeks warm remembering her conversation with him. He had not been with her long, but had left an impression. Not only had he spoken to Thomas, but he seemed truly concerned for her well-being. Through the little she had learned of him, Grace believed he was a good man at heart, and he seemed happiest when doing what was right and helping others when he could.

What really stood out to her, other than once again noticing what a handsome man he is, was how encouraging he had been about the idea of her reading. She was so used to hiding books, she had done so again this morning purely out of habit. But he did not even blink at the idea of a woman reading.

It was exhilarating knowing that she was now in charge of her own life and could do as she pleased. No one at Geffen House had any authority over her—to an extent. Grace was still obligated to attend the different house party events, such as this dreadful afternoon tea. She used to easily converse with large groups of people; while always polite, she was never afraid to speak her mind. Now, though, Grace was so used to keeping her thoughts to herself and spending time alone that she was struggling to engage with the other women and enter the conversation around her.

"Did you hear about Lady Fox?" Lady Wrexham asked gleefully. A murmur went around the room and several ladies shook their heads. "Well," Lady Wrexham began after a dramatic pause, "it's quite the scandal."

What followed next was a tale about how the widowed Lady Fox, still a young woman by all accounts, had fallen in love with and remarried a man who worked as her uncle's law clerk. "A clerk! Can you believe it!" Lady Wrexham shrieked as many of the other ladies tittered around her.

"What is so scandalous about a woman falling in love?" Grace asked before she could stop herself.

"What do you mean what's so scandalous," Lady Wrexham said, clearly offended. "She married far below her station. The man worked for a living and was untitled." This was said as if marrying below one's station and the need to work for a wage were the worst things that Lady Wrexham could possibly think of.

"But if they are both happy, why should that matter?" Grace persisted. "Who does it harm if they are together?" She knew she was pushing her luck, but she felt passionately that when there was real love, nothing should stand in the way of it.

"Who does it harm?" Lady Wrexham said in disbelief, parroting Grace once again. "Why—it upsets the natural order of things" she spluttered. "The class system exists for a reason. It's just not done to upset it in such a manner."

"Would it not be more upsetting to keep two people who love each other separated?" The whole room was looking at Grace as if she were a foreign object. "Would the unhappiness created by separating two people in love for no good reason not have a detrimental effect on far more people than simply upsetting some people's sensibilities?"

Grace knew it was foolish to continue with her current thoughts if she did not want to draw attention and possibly damage her reputation, but she couldn't help herself now that she had started. "What about whomever they ended up marrying having to live knowing their spouse loves another—would that not be harmful? And what about the children who would be brought up in that unhappy marriage? How would life be better for them, growing up in such an atmosphere simply because their parents' marriage was agreed upon under the accepted rules of class?"

Grace was spluttering now, and everyone was looking at her with mouths agape. "You don't know who's harmed when people are not allowed to love whom they will," she said through tears in her eyes. Registering the awkward silence, Grace came back to herself and realized the scene she had just made. Mortified, she could feel herself warming under everyone's stunned gaze. "Excuse me," she said before fleeing the room.

"Well, I never!" Grace heard Lady Wrexham exclaim as she rounded the corner to the balcony for some air.

"Grace . . . are you alright?" she heard Moira say from behind a moment later. Her chest heaving as she tried to slow her breathing and compose herself, Grace felt Moira's gentle hand on her shoulder. "Do you want to tell me what that was all about?" Moira asked.

"I'm sorry," she said, wiping her eyes. "I didn't mean to make a scene. I just get upset with the rules that dictate how we should live sometimes."

"It's fine," Moira said. "I just wanted to make sure you were alright." She peered into Grace's eyes, looking for the truth of what had just transpired. After a moment, she inquired again, "You want to tell me what that was all about?"

Grace took in a deep breath before finding a seat in the shade. Moira followed her and took another chair, still looking concerned. "My husband didn't love me," Grace confessed. "He wanted to be with someone else, and the fact that he couldn't made him miserable. He wasn't the most amiable person to be around, and his unhappiness in turn made me miserable as well."

"Did he mistreat you?" Moira asked, unsure she really wanted an answer.

"No," Grace replied. "He just ignored me. Both our

lives would have been so much better if he would have been allowed to be with the person he loved. But because society wouldn't have approved the match, he married me instead, and both of our lives were ruined." She discovered her cheeks were wet and hastily wiped them before daring to look at Moira.

"I'm so sorry, Grace," she said. "I wish I would have known what had happened to you and how unhappy you were."

"I'm here now," she said, taking her friend's hand and squeezing. "And I apologize for being so awkward. I certainly didn't make any friends in there." An almost maniacal laugh escaped her, with Moira bursting into laughter a moment later.

"Oh, the look on Lady Wrexham's face was priceless!" Moira said between gasps of air. "I will say," she added after calming down, "it was nice to see the Grace I remember coming back."

"It did feel rather nice to speak my mind," Grace agreed. "But maybe I should find a less controversial topic next time."

CHAPTER 12

That evening Moira had planned for yet another dance, and Henry concealed his annoyance with a faint smile. At least she invited additional guests from the neighboring community to join them; he would have more options for dance partners, rather than having to dance with the same hopeful young ladies over and over again. Best of all, Grace would be there, and he was anxious to spend more time with her.

Spotting her across the room, Henry began to surreptitiously make his way her direction, skirting around the edges of the room to avoid being waylaid by potential matches. As he passed behind a potted palm, he heard hushed voices coming from a hidden corner of the room. He would have ignored it, but hearing his name mentioned, he stopped to listen.

"He's always keen to be of assistance," came a female voice.

"Yes, such a gentleman," concurred another woman.

"I'll use that to get his attention. I'll let him know

that Anne is in need of his help and lead him to the conservatory where she will be. Once you see me leave with him, give it five minutes before you bring others over. By that time, I'll have made an excuse to leave, and you will 'discover' them alone together. Make a fuss, and with the witnesses you'll bring, he'll have a hard time arguing his way out of a match with her."

Henry fumed. Based on the conversation and mention of Anne, he knew with certainty the first voice belonged to Lady Wrexham. In no way was he going to allow her to entrap him in marriage with her daughter, but he also didn't want to make a scene. Thinking quickly, he slipped away from behind the palm and made his way toward Reid and Sidney.

"I need your assistance," he told them quietly, glancing over his shoulder to see Lady Wrexham making her way toward him. Turning back to face his concerned friends, Carrington said, "Reid, I need you to quickly take a few people to the conservatory. Sidney, follow my lead." Reid scurried off without question, right as Lady Wrexham arrived.

"Oh, Your Grace," she said while fluttering her fan. "I'm so glad I found you. My poor Anne has twisted her ankle and is unable to walk back to her room. Will you please come with me and help carry her there? I don't think I'm strong enough to support her on my own."

Henry had to fight not to roll his eyes at her theatrics, but he maintained his smile and managed to respond with a tone of concern. "I'm so sorry to hear that Lady Anne is unwell. Of course I'll make sure she is alright." Turning, he looked at Sidney with wide eyes, pleading for his friend to not leave him alone. Sidney must have intuited what was happening because he sent Henry a smirk before turning to him with a serious expression.

"Do you need help, Carrington?" Sidney asked, feigning ignorance. Henry had to suppress his laughter looking at Lady Wrexham's confused expression.

"Will you help me assist Lady Anne?" he asked Sidney. "Between the two of us, I'm sure we can help her up the stairs."

"I don't want to inconvenience you, Mr. Bright," Lady Wrexham interjected. "Surely his Grace can handle a poor slip of a girl on his own, no need for both of you. He certainly demonstrated his strength yesterday when carrying Lady Harcourt." The woman had a glint in her eye as she shared that last tidbit, feeling that she'd cornered Carrington.

"Ah, but with Lady Anne so young and vulnerable, I wouldn't want there to be any hint of impropriety," Henry said, trying not to overplay his hand. If he warned her away now, she would only try such maneuvers again. "Surely a group would protect her if questions were to arise." Henry watched a vein beneath her eye twitch.

"So kind of you to think of her reputation," she said, "but you had no trouble helping Lady Harcourt on your own yesterday, surely Anne is no different." Henry could see Sidney was now flush from laughter, and he had to briefly turn away himself to regain his composure.

"Yes," he said after clearing his throat, "but society is

more forgiving about such rules when it comes to widows, isn't it?"

"So true," Lady Wrexham responded in a distracted manner. "Well, I'm sure it's not that bad, she only turned the ankle a bit. I should be able to get her upstairs myself."

The woman was clearly trying to back out of the situation, but Henry couldn't allow that. He needed to see this through so he could stop such a scene from happening again. "I won't hear of it. We are happy to help and don't want to leave you or your daughter in distress. We simply cannot allow you to fend for yourselves when we may be able to help. Do lead the way, we will follow you."

With a huff, Lady Wrexham turned and began to hustle toward the conservatory. Henry turned to glare at Sidney and whacked him on the arm when the man had the audacity to let his laughter escape. Thankfully, Lady Wrexham was too preoccupied reconfiguring her next moves to notice. A moment later, the three of them entered the room to find Lady Anne conversing with Reid, Moira, and Grace in front of a lemon tree. Lady Wrexham came to an abrupt halt upon seeing others in the conservatory with her daughter and began to turn pink in the face.

"Lady Geffen, Lady Harcourt, Captain Claybourn," she said with a nod while greeting each of them in turn. "Are you here to help Anne as well?"

"Help me with what mother?" Anne asked, looking utterly confused and perfectly healthy. "You told me to meet you here, did you not?"

Henry was relieved that the poor girl was not in on the scheme. While he certainly did not want to marry her, he thought she was a nice enough young woman who was above these kinds of machinations. He noticed that both Moira and Grace looked confused as well, so it seemed Reid had not told them they were on a rescue mission.

Stepping up beside Lady Wrexham, Henry whispered, "I think it's time to cut the act, Lady Wrexham. I overheard you talking with your friend earlier and I know what you were planning." The woman turned bright red and faced away from the others so they could not see her reaction. "Don't worry," Henry assured her, "I'll not call you out in front of the others. But do know that both Captain Claybourn and Mr. Bright are aware of what you were trying to pull," he fibbed slightly.

Before she could respond, he turned and walked out of the room.

"Do you have any idea what that was all about?" Grace asked Moira as they made their way back to the ballroom.

"I have no idea," Moira replied, "but it looked like Lady Wrexham may have gotten what was coming to her."

Upon reentering the ballroom, the dance now in full swing, the women made their way over to Fitz, who was conversing with a frustrated Duke of Carrington.

"Henry, what on earth just happened?" Moira asked. "Something was obviously going on in that conservatory."

"Nothing you need to worry about, it's been handled," he said. "I just need to unwind a bit." Carrington turned toward Grace and extended his hand. "Lady Harcourt, will you do me the honor of dancing with me?"

Grace wasn't sure she would survive such an encounter. She had not danced in years, with the exception of an awkward set earlier that evening with Mr. Stanhope. A dance with Carrington was another thing all together. It would be rude to refuse him, and she liked the idea of being in his embrace again. At that thought, she began to blush. "It would be my pleasure, Your Grace," she said after a pregnant pause.

Taking her hand, he led her onto the dance floor as the current song came to a close. Waiting for the next to begin, Grace felt a bit nervous, but settled when Carrington squeezed her hand. As the first bars of a waltz began, he silently drew her into his arms. She relaxed as the warmth of his body seeped into hers, letting her worries float away with the melody, living in this moment.

He was quiet and still seemed preoccupied, but he was also attentive, examining her face as they turned about the room.

"What are you thinking about?" he asked her. "I can see a question lurking in your expression."

"I admit, I am still curious about what I just witnessed in the conservatory. It seemed something was afoot that most were unaware of, and I'm not entirely sure I was not being used without my knowledge," Grace said honestly.

Carrington sighed and pulled her a bit closer. "I do apologize, my lady. Using you was not the intent, but I can't deny that your presence was helpful. I cannot share more, as I do not want to harm innocent parties involved. Just know all is well."

While still curious, she nonetheless appreciated his discretion. With the matter dropped, she noticed that the duke's attention was now focused solidly on her. As his eyes scanned over her face, she realized just how close they were to one another, and her breath quickened as his presence affected her. Just like yesterday when he had carried her to her room, she felt an instant sense of security.

His eyes slowly drifted up from her lips, which she had licked nervously, and his gaze locked with her own. Her body began to stir to life at the interest she saw in his expression, and she could not deny her attraction to this man. Her fingers itched to run through the slight waves in his chestnut hair, and she forced her hand to remain clasped within his own.

Awareness of everything else in the room began to fade as they stayed locked into one another, and she could barely feel her feet move as he effortlessly glided her about the floor. All too soon, the last strains of the song sounded, and as they stopped moving, she blinked and came back to herself.

"Thank you for a most pleasurable dance, my lady," Carrington said as he bowed before her. Leaning forward, he kissed her fingers before releasing her hand. Even through her gloves, Grace felt the kiss burn all the way from her fingers up her arm. She stood dumbfounded on the edge of the dance floor as she watched him turn back toward his friend, and she knew without a doubt she would be too agitated from his touch to sleep well that evening.

CHAPTER 13

After another early morning ride, Henry felt refreshed and ready for the day. That was quite the feat, considering he had not slept well the night before, his sleep disturbed with dreams of Lady Harcourt. Dancing with her last night had done something to him. Though he had held her before, dancing was different. When he had carried her to her room, he had been concerned for her wellbeing and the contact had been necessary. While it had not left him unaffected, it still had not packed the punch of deliberately pulling her close for a waltz.

Holding her had just felt *right* in a way that he couldn't explain. While Henry was certainly no saint, having been with many women over his thirty-six years, no one other than Grace had ever made him feel this way. Despite his friends' teasing, he was not against the idea of marriage. He had just never met anyone who made him feel compelled to take that step. Being the second son of a second son, Henry never felt pressured to marry and produce offspring, since he would not be the heir to a title. And considering his time away at war, he had no desire to leave a wife or child behind should he perish.

Ever since inheriting his title, however, he felt pressure to find a match and knew his time alone was almost over. His plan had been to settle into his responsibilities before turning his attention to finding a wife. But considering Fitz's words on how a wife could be a partner in his endeavors as duke, and with the draw he felt toward Lady Harcourt, he might be wise to act more immediately. After what could have been a disastrous evening with Lady Wrexham's scheming, he knew he should act quickly if he desired to choose his own wife. With that in mind, he turned his horse over to a stable hand and set out for breakfast.

Rounding the corner of the house, he mounted the stairs to the back porch. Crossing the balcony, his eye was caught by movement near the house. As Henry turned toward the disturbance, he was surprised to see none other than Lady Harcourt herself, sitting in the corner of the balcony and taking in the garden. Just looking at her made a sense of calm wash over him.

"Lady Harcourt, what are you doing up so early?" he called out as he strode toward her. "I was just going to make my way toward breakfast, would you like to join me?"

He offered his arm and hoped she might take it. He wanted to feel her next to him again and, more than that, he wanted to talk with her. The more he sat with the thought of marriage, the more certain he became that he really should take the plunge. And he wanted Grace to fill the role.

Pulling her shawl tighter around her, Grace stood and placed her hand in the crook of Henry's arm, and he immediately felt more settled by her touch, as if she were meant to be with him always, making him momentarily forget which direction he was leading them. It was the same feeling he had yesterday.

"I would be honored to join you, Your Grace. I've been up for a few hours already and I think I could eat an entire platter's worth of food this morning," Grace said.

Jolted back to the moment, he smiled down at her and led the way to the breakfast parlor.

Grace could hardly believe she was once again with the duke. She was more than happy to sit with him and enjoy a leisurely breakfast. They were the first to arrive in the breakfast room for the day and most likely would be the only occupants for a while due to the early hour. Entering the room, she was pleased to see Hudson, the footman who had assisted her before. He looked up from the buffet he was readying for the guests and beamed upon seeing her.

"Good morning, my lady. I hope you are better this morning than when I saw you last," he said with a bow.

"I am. Thank you, Hudson," she assured him as Carrington pulled out a chair for her. Hudson blushed when she called him by name, flattered she had remembered it.

"It is rather early," he said. "I'm afraid we are still setting out the food. Is there anything in particular I can get you?"

Hudson was eager like a puppy dog, and Grace heard the duke chuckle under his breath at his pure earnestness. She smiled graciously at the footman as she made her request. "I'm afraid I woke early this morning and we are inconveniencing all of you with our presence at this hour. I am happy to wait for food, I don't wish to rush the cook, but I would love some strong tea if you could procure some."

"At once, my lady." He quickly turned to do her bidding, but before he could leave the room, she called out his name.

"Yes, my lady?" he said, spinning to face her.

"I think you forgot to ask the duke what he would like," she prompted gently. Grace heard Carrington muffle a grunt of amusement as he sat down next to her.

Hudson's face turned positively scarlet. "My apologies, Your Grace," he said with his head bowed. Turning toward the duke he asked, "Is there anything I can provide for you as well?"

Smiling, Carrington replied, "I would appreciate some coffee when you have the chance, but please do see to Lady Harcourt's tea first."

"Of course, Your Grace." Hudson dipped his head in another brief bow before hustling out of the room.

Carrington looked at her and his eyes shone in

merriment. "That lad is half in love with you, you know," he said. "Not that I can blame him."

Catching her breath, Grace reminded herself that it meant nothing. He was only being polite. There was no way the duke meant that he could feel any kind of affection toward her, let alone a feeling approaching love. And Grace certainly didn't need feelings to interfere with her plans. She had no business feeling anything for any man, as she would hopefully be placed as a companion soon.

Before anything else could be said between them, Hudson bustled back into the room carrying a tray with cups and a steaming teapot. As he set it down next to her, Grace turned to him with an inquiry. "Hudson, do you know the name of the maid who attended to me while I was ill? I should like to thank her."

"I believe it was Miss Molly, my lady," Hudson replied. "Would you like me to find her for you, or to share with her your thanks?" He deftly poured tea for her and then set down a pitcher of cream and a bowl of sugar before removing the tray.

"No, that will not be necessary," Grace said. "I do not wish to disturb her work more than I already have. Thank you for sharing her name. I will be on the lookout for her today so that I may be able to thank her personally."

"Of course, my lady. The cook is just finishing up a wonderful-smelling quiche. I'll bring it up for you both in a moment. In the meantime, there are pastries at the buffet. I will leave you to your tea." He once again bowed and left the room.

Turning her attention back to the duke, she noticed that he was scrutinizing her. "What, is something amiss?" she asked as she patted her hair, trying to assess if anything was out of place.

"You are so kind," he replied, as his quizzical gaze turned to a look of admiration.

"In what way?" she asked, curious as to what had prompted his observation.

"Twice now I have witnessed you take special care to note the service of the staff here," he said. "The other day, even when you were not at all feeling well, you took the time to remember Hudson and to thank him. Then, just now, you inquired about the maid who nursed you. You notice those whom others would overlook, whom others would dismiss as simply providing a service."

Grace was surprised by his observation. "Well, yes," she said slowly, thinking about this from his perspective. "I suppose it is their job, but that does not mean I should not be appreciative when they do it well and it makes my life easier. With Molly, she went above and beyond her normal duties to make sure my needs were met. I'm quite sure that nursing is not a normal part of a maid's duties, and she has enough work to do without attending to me. I owe it to her to acknowledge the extra care she took and to thank her for the service," she finished with conviction.

"As I said," he replied with a soft smile, "you are kind. You are not wrong to observe their dedication and that it should be acknowledged, but many in our class do not think that way. They believe they are superior and should be served. It would never cross their mind to think it extraordinary." He was looking at her with such gentleness and respect that her chest tightened. She was not used to others thinking well of her. In the past seven years, kind words had been few and far between, and now she realized just how starved for them she was.

At that moment, Hudson and another footman reentered the room carrying trays laden with food and a pot of coffee. The haze she had been in while looking at him cleared abruptly with the disturbance, and the momentary spell was broken. Both of them quickly looked away from one another, and Grace busied herself with her teacup.

"May I make you a plate, my lady?" Carrington inquired.

"Please, I would appreciate it," she replied. "I'm not a picky eater, so anything you think looks best . . . Although the quiche Hudson mentioned does sound good, and a croissant with preserves would not be amiss either," Grace said with laughter lurking in her eyes, Carrington smiling as he took in each amendment.

After returning to the table, food now piled before them, Henry repositioned his chair so he was facing Grace.

"I think you are quite remarkable, Lady Harcourt. What I have observed and learned of you in the past few days reinforces my initial good impression. I know you hope to secure your future, and I would like to help you. I think you should marry me."

CHAPTER 14

Silence filled the room, followed by the clatter of a fork.

"I'm sorry, what did you say?" Grace whispered, eyes wide in shock. She leaned backward and desperately clutched onto the napkin in her lap, as if she were somehow lost and it was the only thing tethering her to reality. He recaptured her gaze, searching for any clue as to what she was thinking. Just then, the first of the other guests entered the room, interrupting their privacy.

"I'm sorry," he said, cringing at both the intrusion and his bluntness. "This was not the best moment to bring up such a matter. Why don't we continue our conversation on a walk after breakfast?"

"Yes . . . yes that would be fine," Grace stuttered, staring down at her plate. When another guest wished them both a good morning, she gathered herself enough to respond in kind.

Henry sighed and picked up his fork. He could kick

himself for blurting his thoughts out so bluntly and at such an inopportune time. Grace had seemed quite shocked by his proclamation, and he wanted to make it through the meal as quickly as possible so that they might resume their conversation. He forced himself to make small talk with those around him as the room began to fill with other guests. Grace remained distracted, only picking at her food, and Carrington waited as she finished her meal. The minutes ticking by would be the death of him.

Finally, when he could take it no longer, he pushed back from the table while apologizing to the others still seated. "If you would all please excuse me, Lady Harcourt and I were going to take a walk about the grounds to settle all this food, as it is such a nice morning," Henry explained. He looked over at Grace, her head downcast. Undaunted, he reached his hand out to her.

"That sounds lovely," Mr. Stanhope interjected, angling for an invitation. When one was not forthcoming, he tentatively asked, "Might I join you?" Henry sent daggers Stanhope's way.

At his question, Grace's head snapped up. "Oh, um . . . actually," she said, "there is a private matter I need His Grace for. Maybe we can take a walk later?" Henry admired how graciously she responded while obviously caught off guard. Even though he looked disappointed, Stanhope acquiesced, wishing to appease her.

Grace accepted Henry's outreached hand as she stood up, and they exited the room, her body stiffening. Not until they had put quite a distance between themselves and the house did she break the silence. Stopping abruptly, she turned toward him, not releasing her grip on his arm. "I apologize for speaking bluntly, Your Grace, but what on earth are you playing at?" she said, not able to hold the words in a moment longer. "Are you mocking me?"

"I can assure you I'm not playing at anything. I asked you to marry me in earnest," Henry said.

"I understand that by nature you feel the need to help those around you, but this is too much. I am not seeking a husband. But even if I were, I do not wish for anyone to marry me out of a misguided sense of duty or, even worse, pity."

"My lady, I assure you I do not pity you, nor do I ask out of duty. I genuinely believe we can help one another. May I explain?" he entreated.

Grace held his gaze in search of the truth. She finally nodded in acceptance, and he led her over to a nearby bench sheltered by a thick hedge.

"I'm sorry for how I phrased my earlier proposition," Henry began, "but I stand by it. I believe we can help one another. It would not just be me helping you," he emphasized, wanting her to understand he was not just doing her a favor as she had intimated.

"What do you mean? How would I be able to help you?" she asked with her lovely brow creased in confusion.

"As I am sure you have heard—since gossip is rampant at these types of gatherings—I have not been a duke for long," he admitted. "I was never expected to inherit. I am the second son of a second son, so all of this has been quite a shock. Through a series of unfortunate events, all of those who stood to inherit before me passed, beginning with my older brother five years ago amidst the war."

Her eyes softened as he began to recount how his relatives had perished, leaving him the last in line to inherit. "I'm so sorry," she said. "Were you close with your bother?"

"Yes and no," Henry replied. "Growing up we had been friends, but since he was several years older, we did not mix as much when he went away to school. After university, both of us chose to join the military. We were not in the same regiment, so were in different locations for much of the war. We were apart for two years before he died." He paused for a moment, sadness he rarely allowed himself to feel overcoming him. "I do miss him, but I never really knew him as an adult . . . the person he became. I suppose I mourn that most of all." A hand was placed on his, bringing him back to the present. Looking at Grace, he realized he had become lost in the memories.

"Anyway," he continued, clearing his throat, "that was a long time ago."

"Not so long, really. I lost my father seven years ago and I still miss him every day," Grace said. She gave Carrington a small smile while gently squeezing his hand. "What happened next?"

"Both my cousin, Michael, and my father were ahead of me in the line of succession, so I never contemplated taking the title. When my uncle passed about three years ago, my cousin became the duke. He was eager to find a duchess as soon as he was out of mourning, and became engaged at the end of the next season. He was married between Christmas and the New Year, and we all assumed a new heir would be coming along soon. After the marriage, he and his wife departed for a monthslong honeymoon on the continent. Then a little over a year ago, my father passed away in his sleep." He paused to swallow, looking at Grace. "The very same morning, my aunt received a letter informing her that both my cousin and his new wife had died of illness while abroad. And just like that, I became a duke."

Her eyes were wide as she took in how much loss had accumulated in such a short span of time.

"I'd never been so shocked in my life," he told her honestly. "I had been an army man and spent years abroad fighting on the continent. After Waterloo, I was reassigned to work from the war office in London. My life was fairly simple, but I was content," he explained. "I had purpose, and was doing something for the benefit of my country." Grace nodded as he spoke of his career, seeming to recognize what it had meant to him. "Then suddenly, not only was I grieving my father, but I had to leave my work with the army—the only life I had known as an adult—and a slew of new responsibilities fell on my shoulders. It's overwhelming," he admitted.

Still holding his hand, Grace squeezed it again. "I am sorry you have faced so much loss. I'm sure your life changing so suddenly has been disorienting."

My god, she really was so incredibly kind he

thought again. The warmth of her nature practically radiated off her, and the empathy in her eyes made them shine—emphasizing how beautiful they were. He was convinced he was doing the right thing in offering for her hand.

They grew quiet for a moment, both lost in their own thoughts. "I'm afraid I still don't understand what I can offer you," she said hesitantly.

"I'm lost as the duke," he admitted sheepishly. "I'm still learning what all of my responsibilities are, and I've spent much of the last year travelling to the various properties now under my care trying to learn estate management." He squirmed thinking about the weight of it all.

"It's bewildering when I think of the number of people whose livelihoods are now tied to my own. That sense of responsibility is crushing," he confessed. "I still have so much to learn . . . and when I think about it too long, it makes me want to panic." Henry couldn't believe how honest he was being with her, but her open nature made her easy to talk to. And he owed it to her if she was going to agree to be his wife.

"Yes, I am the grandson of a duke, and was then the nephew and cousin of a duke, so this world is not completely foreign to me. I was raised among the *ton*, but I've been removed from it for too long, and it's quite a different beast when the title becomes your own. I don't think anyone, or anything, can fully prepare you for it."

"I can understand very well the unsettling nature of life taking a sharp turn you were not expecting," Grace offered quietly. "What kind of help do you feel you need?" she asked him.

"An aspect of ascending to the rank of duke which I had not expected, is the rabid nature of those wishing to improve their station." She grimaced slightly at his bold admission, clearly understanding what he meant. "Since coming out of mourning, there are mothers and eligible maidens everywhere I turn," he said with a sigh. "I'm terrified of inadvertently finding myself in what could be perceived as a compromising situation. The last thing I want is to be trapped into marriage with a young woman striving to become a duchess. I barely missed being ensnared into such a situation just last evening," he admitted. He watched her eyes widen in comprehension as she suddenly understood the uncomfortable encounter in the conservatory.

"My friends, who are much smarter than I am," he said with a smile, "have recently pointed out there is an easy solution to some of my problems. If I marry, and soon, I will be able to control choosing whom I want as my wife, rather than the possibility of having someone thrust upon me."

"Sadly," Grace said, "having no control in choosing one's spouse is something I'm all too familiar with."

He squeezed her hand before continuing. "There is also the idea of having a partner for support before going into the next season, someone who can help me navigate the *ton*. And a wife could help me settle into Highland Manor, the main estate in Sussex, as my travels have left me short on time to establish my household and learn proper etiquette."

"I can understand all of that, and I see why you believe marrying soon to be a smart choice," Grace said, "but what I still fail to understand is what makes you think that I would be a good choice for your duchess."

Carrington noticed the familiar, endearing crinkle between her eyebrows. "Why not you?" he said, shrugging his shoulders.

CHAPTER 15

Grace could hardly believe her ears. Had he really said that? *Why not her?* Of all the insufferable things. . .

"Though I've not known you for more than a few days, I genuinely like you, and I feel drawn to you," Carrington insisted. "You have a gentle spirit and a kind heart. And Moira—one of the best women I know —thinks the world of you." She granted him points for recognizing Moira's worth, but this was just too much. How could he not see how wrong she was for him?

"Why not me?" she repeated back to him. "Because I'm not duchess material," she said incredulously, "and I'm not looking for a husband." Finally showing her frustration, she released his hand as she lifted her own in exasperation. "In what way has anything I've shared with you about myself made you believe I am a good match for anyone, let alone a duke! I am technically still in a period of mourning, and I have nothing material to bring to a marriage." She began holding up her fingers as she listed off more reasons. "There are several possible situations where my reputation could be ruined if the wrong people were to speak. And most important," she paused to lift a fourth finger, "I am not known in society and do not move among high or influential circles. A duchess needs connections, and I have none."

"Are you done?" Carrington asked in an amused voice. "I can counter all of those points."

"You are not taking this seriously," she huffed. "I would be poison to you." She squirmed in agitation and began to stand, needing distance to think clearly. His handsome face kept distracting her, and she could not afford to be distracted as she had to make him understand. But before she could flee, Carrington grabbed her hand and gently pulled her back down.

"First, it turns out that, as a duke, I am quite rich. So not having a dowry or widow's portion is of no consequence. Second, you know I had a chat with Thomas, and believe me, he will not be boasting about you to anyone if he knows what is good for him."

While she was reassured by him handling Thomas, he still did not know the truth of her husband's death and the stain it could leave on her reputation should it come to light. She squirmed deciding whether she should tell Carrington.

"What about the fact that I never came out to society and have absolutely no idea what a duchess needs to know?" she asked, delaying a most uncomfortable conversation.

"Are you not the daughter of an earl, and were you not married to another earl?" he said.

"Yes, but that is entirely different," she protested. "I still don't know how to move about in society, as I spent the last six years confined to the North where the dowager countess ran the household. I would not know what to do." She felt a blush creeping up her neck once again. Would she never stop feeling embarrassed by her lack of life experience, even at twenty-five years old?

"It is not different," Carrington replied calmly. "As an earl's daughter, you still existed within the aristocracy, and you have been immersed in the rules of polite society your entire life. I also know you attended a lady's finishing school where you were taught just this type of etiquette, as well as how to conduct the business of a household. Is that not where you and Moira became friends?" He smiled, knowing he made an unassailable argument. She nodded, conceding.

"I don't know why I'm even arguing with you about this," she said, exasperated with herself. "I have no plans to marry ever again, so all of this is a moot point anyway."

He took in a deep breath before looking her in the eye. "From what you have shared with me, I know you do not have the means or support to provide for yourself moving forward," he said delicately.

"And that is why I am trying to find a placement as either a companion or governess," she interjected. "I can look after myself."

"I don't doubt that for a second," Carrington said. "You possess a strength that will always allow you to succeed no matter your circumstances. But why not consider marriage as another option for how you can be secure moving forward?"

"I wish to have control over my own life," Grace shared, hesitating for a moment. "I do not wish to willingly place myself under the command of another."

The look of concern in his eyes as he surmised just how miserable she had been in her marriage forced Grace to look away. "I would never make you do anything you did not wish to. I want my wife to be my partner, not my subordinate." He spoke gently, and she wanted to believe him. Grace could not deny the attraction she felt for him, and if she were to agree to marry him, all of her current stresses would almost immediately be relived. But at what cost?

"Let's say, for the sake of argument, that I were to marry you." Seeing him beam with joy upon hearing these words, Grace interjected, "No, this is hypothetical. I am still concerned that I would harm your image in a manner that would outweigh any good I may be able to do by supporting you." He opened his mouth as if to quibble, but she raised her hand to silence him.

"Let me finish before you try to dispute me again. While I do not like speaking ill of my class, we both know that high society is nothing if not obsessed with reputation, scandal, and watching peers fall from grace. If we were to marry, I would bring nothing to the table. I would only hinder your reputation." Grace paused before adding, "And what will happen when it is discovered that I had only mourned my late husband for four months prior to marrying you? These are not small issues. They may seem petty to us, but they are significant."

Carrington looked at Grace with a raised eyebrow to verify she was done. At her nod, he said, "I hear what you are saying and fully acknowledge the truth in it, but you are forgetting one very important factor."

"And what would that be?"

"I am a duke."

Not understanding what he was driving at, she agreed. "Yes, you are a duke. You are an intricate part of the system that would reject us. How does that change anything?"

"I am a duke," he repeated. "As much as I have resisted it, there are benefits. I am at the very top of the societal structure, and others will do as I say. We've both witnessed this with Thomas. If you agree to be my duchess, we will set the tone together. People may not like us at first, but they will accept almost anything to stay in good favor. And by the following season, we will have been married for at least six months. There will be nothing they can do. Besides, based on what I have learned about you in just a few short days, I know they will come to love you," he said earnestly.

Carrington paused, taking Grace's hand between his. "I am still figuring everything out, and I will admit that I am terrified at the prospect of tarnishing my family's reputation, but I will be stronger with you by my side. We will have time to figure everything out before throwing ourselves at the mercy of the *ton*. I know this was not part of your plans, but I feel this could prove advantageous for both of us."

Grace was breathless after the vehemence with which he had offered his final argument. She was not unmoved by what he had said, but she also could not ignore the voices in her head screaming that she was not worthy and that she did not truly wish to be a wife ever again. Chewing her lip, she said, "I don't know, Your Grace. I truly never planned to wed again. I will need some time to consider your proposal."

"Of course, you may have all the time you need. I know it is a big decision. And please, call me Henry. I think we have moved past formal address, don't you?"

Grace gave him a genuine smile. She was not sure how she had been so lucky as to meet this strong and thoughtful man. And while he had taken her by surprise, he had been nothing but kind to her, so she owed it to him to consider his offer. "Henry then. And I am Grace," she said. "I will give you an answer tomorrow. I know you want to shut down the scheming mamas," she teased.

And with that thought, he beamed.

CHAPTER 16

Grace remained unsettled all afternoon, thoughts tumbling around in her brain. She could not single out an idea long enough to contemplate it rationally, still in shock from Henry's proposal. Accepting Moira's invitation to the house party had been an act of desperation to get away from her in-laws prior to looking for a placement. She never thought marriage would be an option again and was struggling to comprehend Henry's impulsive proposal, though his counterarguments demonstrated foresight.

Softening, Grace thought about how vulnerable he seemed when sharing his fears about not living up to expectations in his new role. He clearly felt the weight of his responsibilities, and she admired his commitment to those who depended on him for their livelihoods. Unlike so many peers, he did not take his people for granted. Henry was a good man who was used to working hard. That was not something she should overlook in her considerations. Grace understood how finding a wife could be beneficial to him, but she was still struggling to see how she was his best option. Who was she to aspire to be a duchess when she had not even been considering being a wife again? She needed to talk with Moira.

Luck was on Grace's side, as she quickly located Moira out on the back patio enjoying some time with her two young children as the other guests participated in lawn games. Moira smiled when she spotted Grace and motioned her to join them.

"Grace, do come and sit with me and my angels before their father steals them away from me," Moira teased. "And where have you been off hiding? I've not seen you all day."

"I've been a little preoccupied with my thoughts. It's been quite a day," Grace replied. "Can I speak with you in confidence about something?"

"Always. Their father is coming to get them for an adventure soon, and we can talk as soon as these little ones have been collected."

"Thank you," Grace said sincerely. "I know you have a lot to organize with this many guests in the house. I can't tell you how much I appreciate you making time for me."

"I always make time for those whom I care about, and that still includes you," Moira responded. "Look, here come the men now."

Fitz was making his way across the lawn toward them, and Grace noticed Henry with him. They must have been returning from an outdoor adventure, as they appeared with hair mussed and faces glowing.

Grace noticed the men had removed their coats—likely due to the heat—and Henry had rolled up his sleeves, revealing his forearms. She was transfixed and watched the muscles and tendons dance under his lightly tanned skin as he gesticulated while sharing a story with Fitz. The men's laughter brought her out of the moment, and she turned away from them to hide her flushed complexion, focusing on the children instead of the duke.

Miles, Moira's eldest, was playing with a young striped tabby cat he found in the barn, and four year old Emily was giggling in her mother's lap. They were both beautiful children who had their mother's coloring, and from what Grace had seen, they were loving and well-behaved. Moira was an adoring mother and played a more active role in her children's lives compared to many of their peers.

Noticing the men approaching, Miles began jumping up and down, much to the displeasure of the cat clutched in his arms. "Uncle Henry!" he shouted. Having had more than enough, the cat leaped from his arms with a hiss, leaving a long scratch across his hand. Miles yelped from pain, his eyes welling with tears as the men reached them.

"What is all this?" Carrington asked gently, kneeling before the boy, and lightly taking his injured hand.

"The kitty hurt me," Miles said, lips trembling. His voice wobbled as he continued, "I was just trying to pet him. I love him, but he was mean to me."

"I'm sorry that you are hurting, Miles," Henry said, comforting the child. "We'll be sure and clean the wound down at the creek when we go fishing and you will feel better in no time." All of this was said with a soothing tone that had a calming effect on Miles. Henry never let go of the boy's hand as he continued to sooth him. "Do you still want to go fishing with your father and I?" he asked. Sniffling, Miles gave an enthusiastic nod. "Good," the duke continued. "But before we go, I want you to go over there and make friends with the kitty again," he said, pointing toward the corner of the patio where the cat now crouched.

"But what if he hurts me again?" Miles asked with more than a bit of trepidation.

"If we treat them with care, animals like cats won't hurt us," Henry told the young boy. "But we have to be gentle with them. Do you think you were as gentle with the kitty as you could have been?"

Miles looked down, shaking his head. In a defeated voice, he said, "Are you upset with me, Uncle Henry?"

Placing his hands on Miles's shoulders, Henry said, "Look at me, Miles." The boy raised his head, noticing the soft expression on his face. Henry continued, "I am not upset with you, and you can never disappoint me, do you understand? But I think this is an important lesson that we need to treat our animal friends with kindness. Animals help us in many ways, and they also give us comfort and love. We need to give them the same love and treat them with care." Miles smiled, nodding in agreement. He wrapped his arms around Henry, who seemed to melt into the boys embrace, then ran off to make up with the cat.

"Well done," Grace murmured, staring at the duke

and feeling a tug at her heart. The sentiment spilled from her before she could think about what she was saying or doing, mesmerized by the scene. He would make an excellent father. Looking up from his crouched position, their gazes locked, Henry beamed at her. Every inch of his stunning face lit up as the smile crawled across his face, and she could not force herself to look away. The moment held as he slowly returned to standing and bowed his head.

"Lady Harcourt, it is a pleasure to see you again," he said.

Fitz cleared his throat, breaking the tension, while Moira looked on wide-eyed. "Well," Fitz said, "we better head toward the fishing hole if we want enough time to catch something for the children's supper." At that pronouncement, Emily slid off her mother's lap and took Fitz's hand. Miles stood in the corner petting the cat as it basked in the sun.

"I want to go fishing, but I don't want to leave the kitty alone," Miles said. "I want to take care of him and make sure he's alright, like Uncle Henry said."

"Why don't you bring the kitty to me, and I'll take care of him while you are gone?" Grace offered. "I have a fondness for cats," she added with a smile.

"Really?" Miles said, now eager to be off fishing with his father and Henry. He scooped up the cat and delivered it to Grace's waiting arms. She snuggled the tabby, watching as the boy scampered over to the men and took Henry's outstretched hand. As she nuzzled the cat's soft head, she could feel the duke's eyes on her, scorching her in their wake. She didn't look at him again, fearing her expression might be too telling, so she turned her attention to Moira.

Before departing, she watched as Fitz leaned over and kissed Moira on the top of her head in a practiced move. Seeing her friend happy filled her with warmth, and she longed for that kind of affection herself.

Moira watched the group amble off with a slightly dreamy smile on her face before abruptly turning toward Grace. Looking like the cat who got the cream, she delightfully exclaimed, "And just what was all *that* about?"

CHAPTER 17

Grace's instinct was to claim ignorance and respond that she didn't know what Moira was talking about. However, that would defeat the purpose of coming out to talk with her about the duke and try to gain some insights on how to proceed. Feeling herself blush, Grace placed a hand on the cat and stroked him gently, gathering her thoughts before explaining.

"Oh, no," Moira said while shaking her head, "don't use the cat to ignore me. I saw that look between you and Henry, don't you try and deny it."

Taking a deep breath, Grace affirmed her friend's statement. "I'm not trying to deny it, I am just trying to figure out where to begin . . . This is what I wanted to talk to you about . . . His Grace has asked me to marry him."

Moira looked as stunned as Grace had felt that morning when the duke had first proposed the idea. Swallowing her nerves, Grace explained to Moira how he had first laid out the prospect that morning and recounted their conversation. She described her fears as well as Henry's justification for the match, and Moira listened in rapt attention. Finally finished, the cat's rumbling purr provided Grace comfort as she waited for her friend's reaction.

"Well, it's not what I believe either of us was expecting, but what an answer to your prayers," Moira finally said. "You now have a solid option for your future, much better than working for another, don't you think?"

"It's all just too much," Grace cried. "What should I do? I understand why he thinks this is a good idea, a wife would truly be able to help him in his circumstances. And I also empathize with his fears about having his choice of partner taken away from him," she said, recalling her own marriage. "But I have no desire to remarry, and even if I did, who am I to be a duchess?"

"Grace, what is it you are truly resistant to?" Moira asked. "Forget for a moment that Henry is a duke. Do you object to him as a man? Do you think you would be unhappy married to him?"

"No, I think he would be quite kind to me, he has been nothing *but* kind and helpful in the short time I have known him." Grace paused, deciding to omit Henry's confrontations with Thomas. "I think he would be a rather remarkable father and husband, and I admire how seriously he takes his role as provider for all those who rely upon his estate management," she said wanting to be fair in her assessment of the man. "But it's not as simple as whether I like him. This would change what I imagined for my future. And even if I did want a husband, forgetting that he is a duke is not possible, it's inherently a part of who he is now."

"So, you do like him?" Moira pressed.

"Yes, alright, I like him." She said, giving Moira what she wanted to hear. "Are you happy?"

Moira sat back in her chair and smiled. "You must admit that he is a handsome man and sharing a life and home with him won't be a hardship. Are you not attracted to him?"

"Moira!" Grace said, blushing again. "I will admit that he affects me, but that is hardly the only thing that matters in a marriage."

"No, but it sure doesn't hurt," Moira said with a smirk. "That look earlier tells me you are indeed attracted to him, and he to you." With her cheeks burning fiercely, Grace was sure she was practically scarlet by now. Serious once more, Moira leaned forward saying, "Look, of course there will be some challenges to such a match when you have unequal standing in society. But Henry makes an excellent argument. As a duke, he will be forgiven for almost anything. Come next season, once the *ton* gets to know you, they will love you as much as we do. And if they want to stay in Carrington's good favor, they will have little choice in the matter but to welcome you and accept your marriage. No, I think the only thing holding you back is your own insecurities."

Moira paused and looked at Grace thoughtfully before reaching for her hand. "I still don't know the story of all you experienced while we were separated, but it's clear to me you have lost your confidence in yourself." Gently, Moira continued, "You said you were not planning to marry again, but with a solid offer, why not take it? Other than my children, my marriage is my greatest blessing. Do you think a life with Carrington could be better than relying on others for a position?"

Moira was correct that Grace was holding herself back, but she was scared. For most, marriage would be a more attractive solution than working for another. But the experience of her previous marriage made her reluctant to enter another, no matter the circumstances. "Not all marriages are as good as yours, Moira," Grace said. "This would not be a love match like you have with Fitz. It would be a marriage of convenience, and I need to consider it carefully in order to protect myself."

"I understand," Moira said gently, "but you yourself have admitted that Henry is a good man. And who is to say that love could not grow between you?" Grace's expression must have shown she found the possibility of love highly unlikely, for Moira continued. "I was not looking for love when I met my dear Fitzwilliam. I was young and wanted to experience some fun before being tied down. I thought for sure I would have at least one full season under my belt before marrying."

Moira now had a faraway look in her eyes, recalling the time seven years ago. "On the face of it, we were also an unlikely match. He was set to inherit an earldom and I was the daughter of a poor baron. He was nearly thirty when we met, and as a young girl of eighteen, I thought he was ancient," she said with a laugh. "But he swept me off my feet and I quickly grew to love him. I believe Henry could win you over in the same way."

"That would be the dream," Grace admitted. "But reality has taught me that that is unlikely. Reservations aside, I can see how he is one of the best possible matches I could hope for." She let the truth of that sink in for a moment, then shook her head. "But reality has taught me differently, and I just don't know if I can relinquish control of my life to a man without knowing his intentions."

For so many years, Grace's life had not been her own. Now that she was no longer bound to anyone else, she did not know if she was willing to legally submit herself to someone else again. As Moira had pointed out, even though marriage was logically the easiest solution for security, Grace was not sure if it was something she could accept.

"Then tell him what you need to feel protected in the marriage," Moira offered. "While this may be a marriage of convenience, you both stand to gain from the union, so go and talk with him. Treat this as a business deal. Negotiate terms that are acceptable to both of you and would allow you not to feel vulnerable entering an agreement. Tell him what you want in return for making his life easier. Embrace the power you would yield as a duchess."

What Moira was suggesting made sense. While

there were several things preventing Grace from feeling comfortable with the idea of remarrying, it was worth a conversation to see what a union between them could be.

What was holding Grace back from truly considering him was fear about what would happen to her if she once again had no say over how she lived her life. But if she could talk over everything with him as Moira had suggested, and he agreed to the freedoms she would ask for, she would be a fool not to consider his offer. Henry was a good man, and a life with him would be far more comfortable than living under employment to another. She needed to trust her own judgment and find the confidence she had lost over the years.

"I think I need to go and find him," Grace said, clear on her next step. "I promised I would give him an answer tomorrow, but I need a few answers from him first."

Grace placed the cat on the ground and stood to go find Henry, but before she made it off the porch, she was stopped by Mr. Stanhope.

"Ah, there you are, Lady Harcourt," he said as he ascended the stairs from the lawn below. "I had hoped I would find you this afternoon. How about the walk you promised me this morning?"

"Oh, yes, of course," Grace said. She had forgotten about Stanhope, her thoughts occupied by the duke. She did not wish to encourage him as he seemed to have grown an interest in her, but it never hurt to be polite, and she could not brush him off again. "Let me just go and grab my bonnet, and then I would be happy to join you on a walk through the garden."

Moira looked on incredulously and shook her head.

CHAPTER 18

Fishing truly was one of the joys of life. Watching Fitz instruct his children on the best way to cast their lines, Henry's mind kept returning to the image of Grace nuzzling the cat. He wanted her to be nuzzling into his neck instead, as she had done while he carried her. It was amazing how she had taken over his thoughts completely in a matter of only days. Guiltily, he realized Miles was calling to him and, based on his tone, had likely tried to get his attention more than once.

Walking down the bank toward the stream, Henry joined the others so he could admire the fish Miles had caught while Fitz helped Emily hold her rod. After another half an hour, the children seemed to be flagging, so they tromped up the bank to rest under a tree where provisions had been left for them by Moira's efficient staff. Henry smiled, his newfound appreciation for the services provided made him recognize and appreciate the prepared food in a way he wouldn't have before and reminding him of Grace. He and Fitz watched as the children gobbled up a snack and promptly fell asleep, bellies full and warmed by the sun. Picking at the last of the summer fruit, Fitz turned his attention to Henry.

"What is going on with you?" he asked. "You've been distracted all day. Come to think of it, you've been acting odd practically since you got here."

"I know, I'm sorry," Henry said. "I've just been making some big decisions." Shifting uncomfortably, he decided to be honest with his friend. "I think you were right the other day about needing to choose a wife sooner rather than later. This morning I asked Lady Harcourt to marry me."

At Henry's pronouncement, Fitz choked on the lemonade he was drinking. "I'm sorry, you did what now?" he spluttered. "You hardly know the lady."

"I know I've not been acquainted with her long, but I do feel like I know her," Henry insisted. "I've had a few long conversations with her over the past few days and I can see what a genuinely good, kind, and strong person she is. I think she would make an exceptional wife and would support me in my work to make improvements to the land and housing on the estates."

"Are you sure you are not just in lust with her?" Fitz said, quirking an eyebrow. "I saw the look you shared with her earlier, you could practically cut the sexual tension with a knife. And from the accounts I heard, you were holding her rather closely on your heroic march across the lawn. Not to mention the way you looked at her while dancing last night."

"I won't deny that I find the lady beautiful and am

attracted to her," Henry said, "but such feelings hardly merit making someone my wife. No, she has many other attributes which I think make her perfect for my duchess."

"Such as?" Fitz prompted. "What do you really know about her? Based on what Moira has told me, she hasn't had an easy time of it and is desperate for some security in her life. You make an appealing target as a rich and handsome duke. Is it possible that she is trying to entrap you just as so many others here wish to?"

"She's not like that," Henry growled. Fitz held up his hands in a sign of submission while Henry continued. "It's true she is not in the best position, but she resisted my proposal and still has not given me an answer. She's convinced she doesn't want to marry again and that she's not a smart match for me if she were to say yes. You know I don't give a fig about appearances," he said to Fitz, who shrugged in agreement.

"She's worried that if we did marry, she'll bring my reputation down because she is not known within polite society," he elaborated. "She doesn't believe she's worth anything because her family and late husband made her feel so through their neglect of her. She's had no one to stand up for her . Even though she's been raised as a lady and is the daughter of an earl, she has lost her confidence that she would know what to do as a duchess. . . But I see her, Fitz. I can tell she possesses the grace and empathy needed to care for the tenants, and she would have a firm command in running a household, if she could only believe in herself again. It takes a strong person not to crumble in the face of what she has had to endure." Once again, Henry felt irritated and sad that poor treatment had made Grace so fully question her capabilities.

"That may be, but you said yourself that she's in a rather desperate position . . . Does that not give you pause?" Fitz asked.

"I understand your hesitation, really, I do," Henry replied, "but she has never asked anything of me other than assistance with one small matter she could not handle on her own, and she has freely shared with me what she sees as her weaknesses." Trying to placate Fitz, he said, "I promise my time with her feels completely different from those who only seek my title. In fact, it seems to be one of the reasons she is reluctant to accept me."

"You're clearly taken with her, and I trust your judgment," Fitz said after a moment. "I'll not push you further on the matter. I just want you to be careful—I don't wish to see you hurt, that's all I'm saying."

"I know," Henry said warmly. "You're a good friend, and I appreciate it when you question me. It keeps me honest. But I know what I feel for her, and I trust her. I want to help her. I want us to help each other."

"Good luck to you then, my friend. I hope she answers you soon and in the affirmative." Fitz clapped him on the shoulder.

"I hope so," Henry sighed. "But I'm worried that her previous marriage has done too much damage and she may truly never want to marry again. I just have to trust that she'll see me as a better option than finding a placement somewhere."

Fitz gave him a sympathetic smile. "Come on, why don't we rouse these little ones and get them back to the nursery for their supper?" he said.

They woke the children and packed up their things, heading towards the house. Fitz carried a sleepy Emily while Henry toted their basket and rods, with a heavy-lidded Miles trotting after them. As they passed the edge of the garden, Henry glimpsed familiar honey-colored hair through a gap in the hedge and diverted for a greeting, only to reel backward. Unprepared for the sight of Grace arm in arm with Stanhope, laughing at something that he said to her. Henry saw red. Without thinking, Henry crashed his way into the garden, cutting off their path.

"And just what are you two up to on this fine day?" he asked, stopping himself from sneering. However, the sentiment still did not quite pass as sounding polite.

Startled, Grace looked at him and recoiled when she saw the barely contained indignation on his face. "Your Grace," she said cautiously. "How did you enjoy your fishing?" The last was said in a natural tone, Grace having rallied her composure. He watched as a veneer of politeness fell over her face like a mask.

The underlying tension of the moment utterly lost on Stanhope, he simply smiled and greeted Henry. "You see, Your Grace," Stanhope preened, "I was able to grab her for a walk after all, as I was not able to join you on your secret rendezvous this morning." Henry had most certainly had enough of the smug, indelicate man and wanted to know what Grace was doing with him, encouraging hopes that Stanhope had obviously been growing toward her since the house party started.

Henry directed a placating half smile in the man's direction.

"Yes," Grace interjected, trying to ease the uncomfortable moment. "Mr. Stanhope discovered me with the countess earlier, and it would have been impolite for me to turn him down a second time, don't you think?" she said pointedly towards Henry, highlighting his rudeness. Looking at Stanhope, she said, "We are having a grand time," but I do think it's time to head back now, as we will soon need to dress for dinner."

"Excellent," Henry exclaimed. "I was just headed back that way myself. I'll join you, as my traveling companions have made their way without me. Do lead the way," he said cheerily. Gesturing with the fishing poles, he motioned them forward toward the house. Stanhope's lips tightly pressed, he submitted to Henry's direction, not wanting to quibble with a duke.

Not more than ten minutes later, the trio had made their way back to the house. It had not been entirely uncomfortable as Grace kept her composure through her irritation and led a stream of polite inquiries directed toward Stanhope, who was clearly delighted by the fact that it was he, rather than Henry, who held her attention on the walk. Henry would let the man have his satisfaction in the belief that he had won the lady's attention over that of a duke. He was sure that in the end, he would be the one with the girl, and that was what mattered.

Ascending the steps of the back porch Grace

thanked Stanhope for the pleasant conversation. "I'll leave you here, I want to confer with our hostess about something before I go in," she said, releasing Stanhope's arm and gesturing Moira's direction across the patio. Stanhope reluctantly left, Grace and Henry watching him disappear behind the French doors. Not more than a second later, Grace whirled around to face Henry with a look of pure agitation.

"What on earth was that?" she gritted out from between clenched teeth, trying to keep her voice down and not draw attention.

"I simply saw you out for a walk and thought it would be lovely to join you," Henry replied.

"You behaved like an arrogant duke," she fumed. "You purport to be uncomfortable using your newly elevated station, but you certainly didn't hold back in cloaking yourself under its mantle just now, when it suited. You acted like a puffed-up buffoon!" she said, causing him to wince.

Henry did not enjoy her accusation of wielding his status for his own gain, but he could not deny that the pronouncement hurt because it hit so accurately.

"I apologize, I stepped in without thinking . . . but I did not like seeing you with him. You should not encourage his obvious fancy for you if you are not going to return his favor, and you should not be entertaining anyone else at this time anyway," he said, growing more fervent with each word as he so passionately wanted her to belong to him.

"You act as if I belong to you," she said in a scarily accurate echo of his own thoughts. Grace spoke with an iciness that made him fearful she may not feel as warmly toward him as he thought.

"Yes, you have made an offer to me," she continued, "but I have not accepted. Even if I had, I am my own person and I do not belong to you. I was out with Mr. Stanhope because he asked me to join him, and it would have been impolite for me to refuse him again. As you may recall, I already put him off this morning so that I might be able to talk to *you*." Her gaze could practically cut him it was so steely. "Furthermore, I resent the fact that you believe I would ever conduct myself in a manner that would lead on any man with whom I did not intend to pursue a possible match."

He stood there, humbled at her beratement, feeling just how wrong he had been inserting himself in the situation and making assumptions based on jealousy. "I apologize if I in any way made you feel that I don't respect or value you," he said, his eyes begging her to forgive him. "That could not be further from the truth."

Looking up toward the sky and huffing out a breath, Grace took a moment before refocusing her gaze on him. "Moira convinced me to be more open in considering your proposal. I had been planning to talk with you about what a marriage between us might look like, but before I could do so, I was waylaid by Mr. Stanhope," she explained. "Now, after that pompous display of arrogance, I'm not sure I still want to have that conversation. Maybe I was mistaken in my assessment of your character," she finished.

"No, please, we can still have that talk," Henry begged. He grasped her hands and was grateful she did not immediately pull away. Dipping his head so he could look her directly in the eyes, he said with all the sincerity he could muster, "I want to have that talk."

Realizing he needed to provide her with proof that he was not usually the man he had just displayed, he told her, "I assure you that if we are to marry, you will always be your own person. Regardless of what the law may say, I would never think that you belonged to me or that I had the right to control you."

Henry paused to gather his thoughts. He was aware that only minutes earlier he had thought he did want her to belong to him, but that was not what he actually meant, and he wanted to find the right words to make that clear to her. But expressing his feelings had never been easy for him.

Speaking slowly, he said, "It's true that should you agree to wed me, I would want you to be by my side, but you would still be your own person. It would not mean as much if you were only there because you felt you had to be. I would want you to belong to me, but only in the sense that you chose to be with me . . . and I would belong to you in return." It was a clumsy attempt at articulating such thoughts for the first time, but he was glad that he had at least tried to make clear what he felt toward her.

Grace's eyes were wide by the time Henry finished speaking, and she was holding on to his hands a bit more firmly. "Fine, we can continue the conversation regarding the possibility of marriage between us, but not now," she said, drawing in a deep breath. "I need tonight to clear my head, and I think we are both too emotional right now for a productive conversation. We can continue this discussion by the roses tomorrow after breakfast. I'll give you an answer then." She released his hands and went inside, leaving him alone on the porch.

Henry smiled to himself, grateful that he had not completely bungled everything with his impulsiveness and protective behavior. There just might be some hope left after all.

CHAPTER 19

Grace's nose was buried in a hedge as she inhaled the sweet, perfumey scent of roses, waiting for the duke to arrive. She had tossed and turned most of the night, not sure what she should do, but needing to make a decision before she went mad. More than anything, Grace wanted to be in control of her own life. The reality was, though, that neither taking a placement nor marrying would fully allow her the freedom she desired, as either situation left her reliant upon another. But she wanted to put aside her fears and look at the situation rationally.

Grace knew her previous marriage was unusual, and it was coloring her views on the institution overall. Not every marriage was happy, but neither were they as neglectful as hers had been. Knowing Henry was a good man, she could see that a union with him would be different; however, the image of an entitled, possessive duke was seared into her mind, shattering the calm she had felt surrounding his proposal after talking with Moira.

Unable to believe the contrast in behavior from the vulnerable man she had seen earlier that day, Grace was unsettled. She believed he had been genuine when he confessed his intimidation taking on the weight and responsibilities of the dukedom. But it seemed he had no trouble flipping the coin and using the title to work for his benefit. He had even used the seemingly unimpeachable believability and influence of a duke as part of his persuasive argument to her when she expressed her fears at the inequality of their stations—implying it was the reason such disparity would not matter and all would be forgiven by society should she accept his proposal.

Grace could accept that argument if he made it in belief that it was the *ton's* own prejudices and hunger for both power and status that would unwittingly work in their favor. It was quite another if he believed that because of his elevated rank he could in fact do, and expected to receive, whatever he wished. Her thoughts tangling in her mind once again, Grace took in one more deep breath of a particularly fragrant rose to calm herself before what would inevitably be a difficult conversation. Hearing a crunch on the gravel path behind her, Grace turned around to face her future.

"Good morning, my lady." Henry stood before her, impeccably turned out. Yet for the first time since she had met him, he did not seem completely sure of himself. Adjusting to his new title, Grace had thought he still knew who he was as a man. It had centered him even in his uncomfortableness as the duke. But standing before her now, Henry did not look her directly in the eyes, making him appear unsure and off balance. Regardless, she couldn't help noticing how stunningly handsome he was. Grace was not sure if she would ever get used to how attractive he was up close, and her hand once again itched to bush a wayward lock of wavy chestnut hair off his brow.

"Should we sit?" He gestured toward a bench nestled within the roses. After they sat, an awkward silence fell over them. "Are roses your favorite?" he asked.

"What?" Grace said, thrown, as she had not expected the question.

"I wondered if roses were your favorite flower, as you requested to meet here . . . I noticed you enjoying them as I approached." He was still speaking a bit hesitantly, as if he was not sure how to address her after their dispute yesterday.

"I would not say they are my favorite flower to look at," she responded, pausing to give it some thought. "That would be either peonies or dahlias, but they are my favorite scent."

Brow furrowed, Henry said, "Has no one ever asked you about your favorite flower before?" as if offended by the idea.

"No, no one has ever needed or cared to know," she told him. Saddened, Grace was reminded of the very reason she wanted to talk with the duke in the first place. She refused to have another marriage where she was once again disregarded. What was needed for her to even consider this step was reassurances from him that she would have control of her own life.

Henry sighed. "I'm sorry . . . for how you've been treated . . . and for my behavior yesterday. I'm still trying to figure out what made me act in such an arrogant and possessive manner. I know we are not well acquainted, but I can assure you it is not normal for me to act in such a way, and I am ashamed of myself." Looking down at his feet, he said, "You were right to call me on my behavior, and I will strive for it to never happen again."

"Why did it happen?" she asked quietly, genuinely curious. Henry looked up at her with a raised eyebrow. "You said you had been trying to figure it out," she added, "and I am interested in what conclusions you have come to. I think it is pertinent information if I am going to choose to bind myself to you."

"That's fair," Henry affirmed while nodding. "I suppose that ever since I asked you to marry me, I've been thinking of you as mine, as if you had said yes. I became protective of you, and when I saw you with Stanhope, I became jealous," he admitted. "I didn't like the idea of your affection being shared with anyone else. Perhaps because I knew that even though I felt as if you already belonged to me, I had yet to actually secure your time and attention." He had a look of deep concentration as he shared his thoughts, and he spoke slowly, finding the best way to articulate them.

"I can appreciate that your instincts kicked in," Grace conceded. "We all react without thinking sometimes, especially when experiencing unfamiliar feelings. And I can understand that after proposing, your view of me may have shifted. But I still take issue with you saying I belonged to you," she persisted.

"I did?" he said, looking genuinely startled.

"Yes, you did. You also said the same thing yesterday when we were arguing about it."

"That's not what I meant," he rushed to say. He stood and began to pace, breathing deeply, taking a moment before continuing. "I think maybe I don't have the right words to explain . . . I don't mean that you would belong to me as if you were a possession, but more so that you would be *with* me. Your affection would be mine because you *gave* it to me, not because I took it or owned it. I would take care of you because you allow me to, and because it would mean something to me. I think when I say you are mine, it's because I feel protective of you."

"You tried to say something similar last night," Grace recalled. "You mentioned that me being with you would not mean something if I did not choose to be there," she said, trying to help him make sense of and communicate his tangled feelings.

"Yes," he said with excitement, still pacing. "There are few people in this world whom I care deeply for and would do anything for, people I have chosen to spend my time with and share my love with. Because they mean so much to me, I would do anything to protect and care for them, regardless of how they feel about me . . . But having those people feel the same way about me, choosing me in return, makes it all that much sweeter. It makes the actions I would take for them mean more. If something is difficult, their choice of me in return makes it easier to bear. Does that make any sense?" Henry's eyes begged for Grace to understand, and she recognized he was not used to expressing his feeling this way.

"I do understand," she said. "To be valued by someone in such a way is a great gift. And you have started to think of me as one of those people?" she inquired, trying further to understand his actions the day before.

"Yes, I think that is what made me behave so beastly. I really do apologize." He looked contrite and a shade embarrassed at having been so open.

His candor helped Grace know that this truly would be a different marriage from her first should she agree to it, but communication alone was not enough to allay her fears at taking so large a step as marriage.

"I greatly appreciate how you have so thoughtfully articulated your feelings," Grace told him. "I can see now what you were trying to say. When you stated that I belonged to you; it was a sentiment of care rather than possession, and I can accept that." Noticing Henry relax his shoulders at her statement, Grace added, "However, before I can consider your idea to marry, there is one other point from yesterday I would like to discuss." She paused, giving his limbs a chance to seize up again. "I was disturbed by the way you used your elevated position almost as a weapon yesterday. You inserted yourself into my conversation with Mr. Stanhope knowing he would not challenge you as you outrank him in social standing." Henry hung his head with her chastisement. "When you proposed yesterday, you brushed off my feelings of inadequacy because as a duke, the aristocracy will be more lenient of what you do. It is one thing to use your position for the greater good and push the bounds of what polite society will accept, but it is quite another to use it as an excuse to behave any way you please.

Henry took in a deep breath as she finished her observation. "You are correct," he said. "Holding such a title carries a great responsibility. Others will now look to me for cues as to how they should conduct themselves. I was acting selfishly yesterday, but I assure you I will not make it a habit to abuse my power." He leaned forward and took her hand again, drawing strength from their connection as he straightened his posture. "If you are still willing to consider my offer, I would hope that you'd challenge me if my attitude became inflated, or I were ever acting unjustly."

Grace smiled at the idea that she would be able to address him freely in the future. "I am still willing to discuss the possibility of a marriage between us, but first I think it is only fair that I explain a few things to you which might better explain my feelings, just as you have done this morning."

CHAPTER 20

Henry felt lucky that Grace was still willing to entertain the idea of becoming his wife after he had so spectacularly erred by acting without thinking yesterday, knowing she was wary of the idea of another marriage. After a sleepless night of uncertainty, he feared he had scared her away for good. Now, even if apprehensive about what she would say, he was more than willing to hear anything she wanted to share.

"I think I was so caught off guard when you told me that we should marry yesterday that I reacted from a place of fear," she started. "While there are still many legitimate reasons why I am not the most obvious match for you, I trust that when you tell me my lack of social standing does not matter to you, you are being sincere." Henry smiled at her trust, considering it a step in the right direction. "I also concede that given the nature of the *ton*, everything I see as a deficit would not necessarily hinder your ability to be influential in the peerage."

Hope began to fill Henry's chest, and he took her hand. Though optimistic, he was not yet sure of victory as he watched her struggle to find the right way to express herself. Adjusting on her seat, Grace pulled her hand back from his. Her nervous movements conveyed it was not easy for her to speak up for herself, and he admired her for doing so anyway. "What is holding me back from accepting you is fear over what my life might be like if I were to once again bind myself to another man," Grace said, wringing her hands. "I explained a bit about how my marriage was not a happy one. It was certainly not a love match, and while ours would not be either, I do believe that you at least respect me and will look out for my best interests."

"That is true," he reassured her. "I have deep respect for you, and I admire your strength." Grace sent a small smile his way at his admission.

"I need some clarity on what you would expect from me as your wife, and I would like to share some of my own hopes with you."

"That is more than fair," Henry conceded. "Are there particular things that are important to you? What would make you comfortable to move forward?"

She took a deep breath to steady herself before making her requests. "I need to know that you would allow me the freedom to live as I choose—and would grant me the authority of head of the household." Grace exhaled forcefully, and Henry could tell it had been hard for her to speak so plainly.

Hesitantly continuing, Grace shared, "In my

146

previous marriage, I was not allowed to do anything . . . I had no purpose, and I felt like a bird in a cage."

"Like reading?" Henry asked, recalling how she had reacted when he found her in the library. She nodded, not meeting his eye.

"I need to know I would be allowed to run things the way I think best, and to spend my free time as I desired." Lifting her gaze to meet his, Grace said firmly, "If I wish to garden or spend all day reading, I will be able to do so, as it will have no impact on what you do or how you run the estate." The request clearly came from a place of deep hurt from how she had previously been subdued, and his heart ached at how she must have been treated before that she felt the need to make such things clear.

"I have absolutely no wish to control your movements or actions," Henry reassured her. "You asked what I expect from a wife." Grace nodded, a look of apprehension creeping back onto her face. "While *expect* would not be my word of choice, as it seems too harsh," he noted that she smiled slightly at that, "I would *wish* for a wife to help me by ensuring my household runs smoothly. I have no problems with you taking complete control in that area, in fact, I welcome it. It would lift a huge burden off my shoulders if I knew the household staff were being taken care of." Henry noticed her visibly relax at his words.

"Beyond that," he continued, "I should like a partner and companion to accompany me when I attend political or social functions, though I would never demand your presence. As for how you spend your time, your life is your own, as long as your actions cause no harm."

Grace smiled fully, and Henry felt they were coming close to an agreement.

"You promise you are not intimidated by a woman who likes to read? You don't feel women are harmed by knowledge?" her face was anxious as she awaited his reply.

"Grace, you may read to your heart's content. Highland Manor's library has enough books to keep you occupied for a lifetime." Henry was grateful he had a library to offer to her, she deserved to have the joy of unrestrained reading and learning if that is what she desired. "I dislike the idea that women should not be educated. I think those who promote it are small minded and fearful of what could happen should women challenge the accepted rules which keep them second-class citizens in our society." If he had thought her beautiful before, the way her face lit up as he defended her right to learn put all he had known before to shame.

"What other fears are holding you back?" he gently prodded, "I want to make sure your mind is at ease."

Unsettled again, she looked down to where her hands were clasped in her lap. Henry knew whatever she was going to say must be serious, but he was distracted by how lovely she looked with her full eyelashes fanned across her cheeks when she angled her head down in such a manner.

"I understand the duties of a wife," she started hesitantly, "but as I have known you less than a week, I would like to ask you . . ." She paused, unable to utter the words.

"What is it?" He asked gently. "You can ask me anything. This will only work if we are open and honest with one another."

Raising her eyes to his, she spoke boldly. "I don't wish to have marital relations with you right away. I would like some time to get to know you better before we . . .before I will be comfortable sharing myself with you in that way." Her cheeks blazed at the topic. As surprised as he was by her unexpected request, he could not help but be captivated by the blushes he was coming to love.

"That is not unreasonable," he assured her, answering carefully, aware of her vulnerability in making such a request. "I certainly want you to feel comfortable when we come together as man and wife. I would never force myself on you. However, I will need an heir, so this agreement could not last indefinitely."

Grace seemed calmer now that he had not immediately disregarded her request. "I know an heir is part of the bargain when marrying a lord," she responded, having composed herself. "I am happy to place an end date on a period of getting to know one another. Are you willing to allow a month?"

He was surprised she had asked for such a short window of time. While he was more than ready himself to get the beautiful woman into bed, he truly did want to make sure she would be a willing partner. "A month seems reasonable," he agreed, surprised at the brevity. "I am happy to check in with you after a month has passed, and reassess if necessary," he offered.

"Thank you, Your Grace," she said with a sigh of relief and a smile. He would do anything to earn more of those smiles. "Then I think we are agreed. I can hardly believe I am saying this, but yes, I will consent to marry you."

Henry beamed; he couldn't help himself. "Thank you for trusting me with your care," he told her. "I know you have hesitations, but I truly believe you will make an incredible duchess." Henry had no idea how he had been so lucky to stumble across this kind, stunning woman. Somehow, he had managed to gain her confidence and agreement to become his wife. Without thinking, he asked, "May I kiss you?"

Her eyes widened, and after a moment, she slowly nodded. He cautiously drew closer to her, unhurried, raising his hand to her cheek and cradling her face as he looked intently into her eyes. They spoke several emotions at once: hope, curiosity, trepidation, but also longing and desire. While he wanted to devour her, he restrained himself, barely moving his head forward across the gap that remained between them. Brushing his lips gently against hers, the only thought that rang through his head was *"finally."*

Grace did not react at first, her posture still rather stiff, but as he made another brief pass over her lips, she softened. Pressing his lips more firmly against hers now that she seemed more receptive, he brought his other arm up to wrap around her shoulder, pulling her closer, flush against his chest. When she brought her own arm around him to return his embrace and leaned into the kiss, it felt as if he had come home. A warmth started to spread all throughout his body, and his fingers seemed to tingle where they touched her cheek. After a fourth, and more prolonged press of his lips, he gradually pulled away to give her a bit of space, keeping his arm around her, unwilling to completely lose their connection. Appearing lost in the moment, Grace closed her eyes and pressed her cheek further into his hand.

"Grace," he said reverently, "what you do to me."

She reopened her eyes and looked at him as if she did not know how to process what had just happened, her lips now reddened from the kiss and slightly parted. She lifted a hand to her face and pressed her fingertips to her lips. "I've never been kissed before," she said in awe.

Stunned, Henry stared at her in shock. "How is that possible?" he asked. "You were married."

"Yes, but he never kissed me." She answered as if there was nothing strange in the fact that a woman who had been married for six years had never received a kiss from her husband.

"Not even on your wedding day?" he pressed, unable to believe what he was hearing. How had any man been able to resist her? "He never kissed you in the marriage bed?" he couldn't keep himself from asking.

She was once again blushing, but he could not revel in her embarrassment this time. What an utter waste of a man she had been married to if he would not cherish her and show her affection. He now understood the significance of her final request. If her husband had never kissed her, he could only imagine what an uncomfortable place their marriage bed must have been.

"I know it probably sounds strange that a widow of five and twenty would not know how to kiss," she said quietly, "but I'm glad you were my first."

His heart swelled at her admission. Composing himself, he took her face between his hands and looked her straight in the eyes so there would be no misunderstanding what he meant to convey to her. "Darling, I'm sorry you had to give so much of your life over to a man who clearly did not deserve you. If he did not show you affection, that is because of his own problems and is no reflection of you." He could see the insecurity in her eyes, so he continued, "There is nothing wrong with you, do you hear me? You are grace and beauty personified and I am lucky you have agreed to be mine—I mean my wife," he said, quickly correcting himself and seeing her smile at his fumble. "I am beyond honored that I was the first man to give you a kiss," he continued. "It is only the first of many," he promised, "and I'd be even more honored to be the last person you kiss."

Her eyes welled with tears, and she surprised him once again when she replied, "Will you please kiss me again now?"

CHAPTER 21

Grace was overwhelmed with sensation and didn't know how to respond. All she knew was that Henry's kiss was warm and gentle, and it was making her body awaken in ways she had never experienced. At her request, he immediately wrapped his arms back around her and crashed his lips onto hers. Just as before when he had carried her, she felt completely safe and cared for in his arms, allowing her to lose herself in the sensations his kiss was stirring. He moved his lips against hers with more force than before, though not aggressively, and sparks of pleasure shot down her spine.

When she felt his tongue trace her lips, she was not completely surprised. One of the girls at Lady Evelyn's had kissed a few of her neighbor boys before starting at the school and explained how they would stroke their tongues into her mouth. At the new sensation, Grace opened slowly and was stunned at how good it felt when his tongue touched her own.

A small sound escaped her before she could prevent it, and instinctively she responded by tentatively moving her own tongue against his. Henry groaned into her mouth, deepening the kiss even further. Just when she felt she might faint if she did not get more air, he eased the kiss and separated his lips from her own. Trying to catch his breath, he leaned his forehead against hers and let out puffs of air from his nostrils as he regained his composure. Overwhelmed with feeling, she leaned her head against his strong chest and buried her head into the place where his shoulder met his neck, breathing him in.

He held her tight and kissed her temple. "Thank you for trusting me," he whispered into her ear, his voice gravelly. "I'm glad that you trust me enough to let me have your kisses."

She pulled away from his embrace and tried valiantly not to blush but failed utterly. While she still did not want to rush intimacy with him, she was grateful to realize that sharing relations with him might not be such an ordeal. She had never enjoyed coupling with her late husband, but blessedly he only came to her infrequently. The way her body had felt alive when Henry kissed her was a new, pleasurable feeling. It was the reason she had been bold enough to ask him for a second kiss.

"I do trust you," she reassured him, finally looking at him now that they had pulled apart, "and I am grateful you are willing to give me time and let intimacy grow between us." He smiled at her, his eyes brighter than normal, like the sun breaking through the clouds and glittering off the gray waves of the North sea. His hair was slightly mussed from when he had leaned into her, and this time she did not stop herself from reaching up and brushing it off his forehead, smoothing it back into place.

"I suppose we had better go and inform our friends that we are to be married," he said after a minute. "Then we'll need to make some decisions about when the wedding should be." Standing, he held his hand out to her and she took it. Drawing her to his side, he kept hold of her hand as he led her back down the path toward the house.

Passing a group of late-blooming peonies, he stopped and snapped one off, handing it to her. "For you. I believe you said it was one of your favorites." It was a small gesture, but he had no idea how much it meant to her. No one had shown her such thoughtfulness since her beloved father had died. Not realizing the effect of his gift, Henry tucked her hand into his arm and continued down the path as if nothing out of the ordinary had occurred. Grace turned her head away from him and wiped the tears from her eyes before he could notice, keeping the sweetness of the moment for herself.

Moira was overjoyed when they shared the news with her and Fitz. "Oh, I am so happy for you!" she exclaimed through tears while throwing her arms around Grace. Fitz, though calmer, had a large grin on his face while he shook Henry's hand and clapped him on the shoulder. Moira insisted on opening a bottle of champaign, though it was not quite midday yet, and assured Grace that the other guests could fend for themselves for a while as she celebrated with the new couple. Soon Henry's other two best friends entered the drawing room, and he shared the news with them. While the two men were surprised, both immediately congratulated him and then turned toward Grace to get to know her better.

She had met the gentlemen at the opening dinner a few days prior, but so much had transpired at the house party that she really had not spent time with either of them. Henry stepped forward for further introductions.

"Grace, I know you have been at a few meals and dances with these two yahoos, but let me introduce you more formally." Gesturing toward a man who could almost have passed for his brother in looks, albeit taller and broader in stature, Henry said, "This is Captain Reid Claybourn. Reid was the commanding officer who led my unit most of the time while I was fighting on the continent, and he is now an MP for Dorset, and the heir apparent to the Earldom of Weston."

"For my sins," the captain muttered under his breath, seemingly displeased at the idea of one day being the earl. He came forward to take Grace's hand and bowed. On closer inspection, she recognized that while his coloring was close to Henry's, his hair was a shade darker, and his eyes were a deep brown rather than Henry's gray.

"It is a pleasure to meet you in a more personal nature, my lady, and I look forward to getting to know you. Being good friends with Henry, I'm afraid I will now be a bit of a fixture in your life as well." Grace laughed at his sentiment and was pleased by his easy nature.

"And this," Henry continued, "is Mr. Sidney Bright, a friend from my school days whom I met through dear Fitz. His family resides on the neighboring estate to Geffen House." A tall, thinner, yet still well-built, man stepped forward. She had sat next to him at dinner that first evening, but as Mr. Stanhope had monopolized most of her attention, she felt she was truly seeing him for the first time.

Sidney had a mischievous smile on his face that highlighted his unusual coloring. His hair was a blend between blond and red that made it impossible to call him either one or the other. His blue eyes were intensified by a face liberally covered in freckles, making him appear younger than his age of mid-thirties, Grace assumed, as he was a school companion of Henry's. Instantly, she could tell by his smirk the man was a lot of fun but could also be trouble.

"I would offer you good luck," he said, stepping forward and grasping her hand, "you'll need it when dealing with that grump." He smiled teasingly as Henry reached out and swatted him on the back of the head. "Oof, suppose I deserved that," he said, continuing to grin. "But truly, congratulations. You could not have decided on a more noble or trustworthy man."

Grace smiled at both of them and realized that the room was now filled with the group Henry had spoken of earlier, the ones whom he chose and would do anything for. It was obvious that they all cared for and chose him in return, just as he had desired. She felt honored that he already felt enough for her to consider her one of them. While yesterday's incident with Mr. Stanhope was still unsettling, she began to understand it through Henry's eyes, and saw it in a different light.

Passing around champaign, Moira turned the conversation toward the wedding. "Of course, we must have the ceremony here," she said excitedly, eyes bright. "I assume you want to do it quickly, so we can do it the day after the house party concludes and the other guests have departed."

Henry looked at Grace while nodding. "That works for me, assuming I can get a special license," he answered. "Grace, are you alright with moving so fast?"

"Yes," she reassured him. "I will be quite happy not to return to the new Earl of Camden's residence." The thought made her smile. She began to feel the tightness in her shoulders ease for the first time in years as it sunk in that she would never need to rely on that horrid man or her own unfeeling cousin again.

"Is there anyone else you would like to be here?" Moira asked. "Invitations would need to be sent out right away. Sidney, Reid, you are able to stay a day or two longer, are you not? Oh, and we must see if Angeline would be able to come," Moira rattled on, not waiting for answers to her questions.

At the woman's name, Sidney's head popped up from the plate of sandwiches that had been brought in. "Angie? How is she?" he asked. "I've not seen her in a while, will she want to attend?" He seemed genuinely concerned.

Grace leaned toward Henry and asked in a low level only he would be able to hear, "Who is Angeline?"

"Angeline is Fitz's sister," Henry answered. "She lost her husband quite suddenly and tragically about a little over a year ago. Since then, she has not come out for many social events, even those with only family and close friends. I hope she will come, she's a lovely person," Henry explained while offering her a soft, sad smile.

"We'll ask her, love," Fitz said, leaning over to kiss Moira on the temple, "but such an occasion might still be a bit overwhelming for her, so we should not count on her presence." Moira and Fitz both seemed sad but resigned to the idea. Grace noted the way Sidney bowed his head before the others could see his devastated expression.

CHAPTER 22

The rest of the day passed by in a blur. While Moira whisked Grace away to go over details of the wedding breakfast and to arrange for a dress to be altered, Henry called for Smyth to help him make plans.

"I am delighted at the news of your impending nuptials, Your Grace," Smyth offered with a smile, flooring Henry at the rare sighting. Smyth was a serious man who usually took his job caring for the duke with utmost gravity. "Everyone at the manor was hoping you would find a good woman to bring home as our duchess." Henry became overwhelmed thinking about his staff's reaction. He had been the duke for only a year and had spent so little time at the manor that he did not realize the staff was so affected by what he did. It was another area where he would need to continue to grow, and now, thankfully, he would have Grace to help him. Thinking about the way she had been generous in her praise to the staff here at Geffen

House, he knew they would be well taken care of upon his return home.

Informing Smyth that he would be leaving for London tomorrow to secure a special wedding license, Henry received a long list of preparations from Smyth to pick up on his way out the door. As it would be a quick trip, he did not need Smyth to accompany him, but the man fretted at making him a wedding ensemble out of the clothes he already had at Geffen House. Henry could honestly care less what he was wearing as long as he was presentable to Grace, but he would not let Smyth know. He had no desire to belittle the man's occupation or his excitement over clothing him for such an occasion. List in hand, Henry went to find Reid.

He found him in the library, intently reading the latest newspaper from London, which was hardly a surprise. Hearing Henry enter, Reid lifted his head before folding the paper and grunting. "The unrest among those in the trades and the serving class is growing. If Parliament won't agree to extending more rights and easing taxation, I fear violence may soon break out."

"Do you think it has become that serious?" Henry asked, brow furrowed.

"I do. That's why I was working so hard to get something, anything, through the House of Commons before the last session came to a close," Reid sighed in frustration. "We'll have to deal with this first thing when Parliament reopens. I'll bring you up to speed on what we need to have approved in Lords to help us out in Commons, but that will be a much harder battle, as it's the peers who feel most threatened by change."

"Let me know what you need, and I'll champion it," Henry told him. "But first, I need your assistance. Will you accompany me to London tomorrow?"

"Of course, I was going to offer anyway when I saw you at dinner," Reid said with a smile, summing up why Reid was such a good friend. With dinner in mind, both men headed out to join the others.

Dinner proved to be a rather interesting affair as Fitz made the announcement of the engagement between Henry and Grace. There were several shocked faces before common etiquette was remembered, and hearty congratulations were offered all around. Stanhope looked a bit crestfallen at losing his chance with Grace, but he did not interfere with others celebration. There were a few young ladies who looked sad, and Lady Wrexham had a particularly sour expression on her face. Overall, however, people did genuinely wish them well on their impending union.

The next morning, Henry said goodbye to Grace at an early breakfast, then mounted his horse and rode off toward London with Reid. He could still hardly believe that Grace had consented to marry him, but in just a few short days, she would become his wife.

Grace willed away a headache that was trying to take hold while Moira pestered her about decorations for the wedding to spruce up the chapel at Geffen House.

She loved Moira dearly and was truly grateful that she was hosting and planning the wedding for them, but the level of detail involved was exhausting. "Since it will be such a small group, could we not hold the ceremony in your formal parlor rather than the chapel?" Grace asked. "It's just so grand and cold in the chapel, it might be nice if the space were more intimate, and then there would be less to decorate."

"Well, I suppose we could, if that's what you really want," Moira replied, "though that's not very majestic."

"I know it might disappoint you, and I so appreciate your love and enthusiasm for the wedding, but I neither need nor want something grand. This will be a second marriage for me, and it is a marriage of convenience after all."

"Oh, come now," Moira tutted. "I know it's too soon for love, but don't give me that 'marriage of convenience' nonsense. I can see that the two of you care for one another," she said. "Henry has stars in his eyes when he looks at you, and in return, his looks make you blush. I know there's deeper affection than you want to let on."

Recalling their kisses near the roses, Grace felt her cheeks heating even now. "There, that!" Moira exclaimed, looking at the rosy hue overtaking her neck and face. "Whatever were you thinking of just now to bring that on?"

"After I agreed to marry him, Henry asked if he could kiss me, and I allowed it." Grace shared.

"Based on that blush, I would wager it was a good one," Moira smirked.

"I have no further comment on the subject," she said with finality, much to Moira's amusement.

Just then, Hudson entered the room holding a large box. "A delivery for you, my lady," he said, bowing before Grace.

"For me?" she exclaimed. Taking the box from the footman, she said, "I wonder what it could be, or who it could be from. Thank you, Hudson." The footman beamed at her before bowing a second time and leaving the room.

"Is there a note?" Moira asked, peeking over Grace's shoulder. "Look, there, attached to the side of the lid."

Grace pulled out the note and scanned to the bottom for a name or a signature. "It's from Henry," she said. Moira elicited a sigh at the gesture, while Grace returned to the note.

My Dear Grace (or should I say, My Dear Duchess?),

I should return with Reid tomorrow, as I was able to get the license this morning. Do not be cross with me, but this was an instance where I fear I needed to use my influence as a duke in order to move things along. As the end result is undeniably for the greater good (that result being our union), I regret nothing.

I am sending a few things ahead from London. I hope you enjoy them and know that I am thinking of you in my absence. I am eternally grateful that you have chosen to be mine.

I will see you tomorrow (though not soon enough),
Yours,
Henry

Her curiosity piqued by the sentimental and personal nature of the note, she made quick work of opening the box. Inside was a beautiful bouquet of large, lush dahlias with a note attached to the stems: *Such a lovely lady deserves to have her favorite flowers not only known but provided whenever possible.* Grace was touched by the effort Henry had made to procure the flowers. He would need to visit a hot house as it was too early for dahlias to be in season. Next was a small, ornate cut glass perfume bottle with a note around its neck: *A woman should always have her favorite scent available.* Releasing the stopper, she inhaled the purest aroma of roses she had ever smelled outside of the real things. Already emotional that he had remembered their conversation in the garden, and that he had even thought to ask her favorites in the first place, she began to tear up.

It was the final item, however, that broke her. She pulled a book from the bottom of the box, and as she opened the front cover to read the title, a note fluttered out. Before picking up the note, she saw that the book was a collection of Mary Wollstonecraft's works, including *Thoughts on the Education of Daughters* and *A Vindication of the Rights of Woman.* Tears streaming down her face, she picked up the note: *Every woman has the right to an education and to be the mistress of her own life. I choose you, but you are your own. I hope you will enjoy adding this to our library.*

Noting Grace's emotional state, Moira, who had given her some space to open the gift in semi-privacy, asked, "What's wrong?" She picked up the book and looked at Grace in confusion. "Why has a book upset you?"

"Nothing is wrong," Grace said, "and I'm certainly not upset. In fact, I'm quite happy."

Studying the book, Moira asked, "But what does it mean?"

"It means that he sees me," Grace responded. She could not remember the last time someone had recognized her for who she truly was or treated her as more than an afterthought. Henry had not only listened to her, but he had heard what she said.

Overcome, Grace realized that she was marrying a truly wonderful man, and she may be in danger of falling in love with him after all.

CHAPTER 23

In the end, it was a lovely but simple wedding. Henry and Reid had returned from London as the house party concluded, and the next day had seen them married. It was a small gathering with Henry's three best friends, Moira, and Angeline joining them after all. Fitz was delighted to see his sister, obviously caring deeply for her, and her appearance allowed him to relax. Happily, Thomas left with some of the guests as the party dispersed and did not attend the reception even though he was family to the hosts.

Sitting at the table with everyone and enjoying the wedding feast, Grace marveled at how her life had changed within the span of a week. While much of life with her new husband was still unknown, and past experiences made her cautious, she suspected her life might be much more pleasant moving forward.

The afternoon before, she had composed two immensely satisfying letters that would be sent out with the days post. The first was to inform the new

Lord Camden that she had remarried and would not be returning to the Camden residence in London. Grace relished writing the first letter, but the second letter was a bit more difficult. She had always hoped to maintain at least a cordial relationship with her own cousin. Yet, when she had essentially been told she was no longer his problem after her husband passed, she had shuttered any remaining hope regarding her relatives. So, it did prove satisfying to inform Edwin that she had married well, and would not need anything from him moving forward. Seeing the letters leave the house this morning provided a sense of closure on that chapter of her life. And now, sitting at a table next to her new husband, she was anxious to see what this next chapter might entail.

"You are not eating, are you well?" Henry asked Grace, noticing her untouched plate of food. His inquiry quickly snapped her out of her thoughts, and she shook her head to clear it before answering.

"Yes, I am well. Just a bit overwhelmed. I was thinking about how quickly my life has changed in such a short amount of time."

"I hope you do not regret your decision?" he asked, his tone uncertain.

"No," she reassured him. "I just never imagined this would be the outcome of accepting Moira's invitation to join the party here at Geffen House."

"And I was not sure you would agree to marry me once I asked," he replied. It was said lightly, almost teasingly, while placing his hand on hers.

Starting to blush, as seemed to be her response to

everything these days, she said, "Yes, I'm sure you think me foolish for hesitating when I was clearly in something of a desperate situation. I know the world will think it obvious that marrying a duke would be a better situation than setting out to work, but when faced with an option to marry again, I discovered that financial and social security is not what really matters to me in the end."

"I'm sorry for teasing you," he told her seriously. "I did not mean to make light of your decision. I like knowing that you did not merely settle for me . . . that you chose me after consideration."

"I'm happy with my choice," she affirmed. "You have shown me that you care for my well-being and that this marriage will be different, and for that I am grateful."

Henry grinned at her response, and it could have lit the room. "Have I told you how beautiful you look today?"

Grace was taken aback by his statement as she was dressed rather plainly in a cornflower blue silk dress of Moira's that her staff had assisted in converting to fit Grace's slightly smaller frame. Though it highlighted her eyes, there had not been enough time to finish the gown with many flourishes. Grace was grateful as she preferred a simpler gown, but she knew it was not in keeping with current trends. "Thank you," she said, not knowing what else to say.

"And," he said, leaning in to whisper in her ear, "you smell lovely. Like the freshest rose." She shivered at his closeness. His breath made the fine hairs at her temple dance, tickling her cheek. She felt him inhale at the crook of her neck as he pulled back, and she immediately missed his warmth and nearness.

When she felt she could speak again, Grace said, "Thank you again for the perfume, I love it. I love all of the gifts you sent me. No one has shown me such consideration in a long time, and I appreciate that you remembered what I shared with you. I can't tell you how much that meant to me. It's more valuable than the items themselves."

"And that is why I think you will be a wonderful duchess," Henry said affectionately. "Others would only care about and be distracted by the material comforts that can come from holding such a high position, but you don't care about those things, only the good you can do with them."

Grace was flattered that he saw her that way, and she was not sure she had ever felt so seen or understood in her life. When she had received the Wollstonecraft book from him, she knew that it was his way of telling her he had heard her fears about entering into marriage again. He would allow her to be her own woman, valuing what she had to offer through the work she would do as a duchess.

The rest of the day passed enjoyably. Moira's kitchen staff had risen to the occasion and presented the group with a veritable feast. After several long hours spent around the table in laughter and conversation, the final bottle of wine was emptied and the events of the day began to catch up with everyone. Making her excuses, Angeline was the first to leave the party for the evening, and Grace noticed how Sidney's eyes followed her out of the room. She wondered if there was more than just friendly affection there, but she did not know either of them well enough to assess the situation.

Stifling a yawn, Henry let out a low chuckle as he observed her. "It's been a long day," he said, "we should probably say our goodnights as well." She thought his phrasing a bit odd, as he had agreed to give her some space before they would conjugate their marriage. There was no reason for them to leave together, but she agreed and they walked upstairs together after sharing thanks and goodbyes with their friends.

Grace made quick work of divesting her wedding gown with the help of a maid and, after donning her night rail, took a few minutes to enjoy brushing out her hair. She had always loved this little luxury and savored the sensation of the bristles massaging her scalp after letting her hair out of its many pins for the day. Needing rest, as they were leaving for Somerset tomorrow and it would be a long journey to Highland Manor, she set aside the hairbrush with a sigh. Just as she was about to pull back the covers of her bed, she was startled by a knock on the door.

Wrapping her dressing gown back around her, she opened the door and was shocked to find Henry in a robe. "What are you doing here?" she spluttered. "I thought you had agreed to give me time?"

"And I fully intend to honor that agreement," he said.

"Then what are you doing here?" she asked, bewildered.

"Let me in and I'll tell you."

She wordlessly stepped aside to allow him in, puzzled as to his presence. Once he was standing next to the fire, she shut the door and made her way over to him, clutching her dressing gown closed.

"I promise I am not here to make physical advances," he reassured her, picking up on her unease. "I fully intend to allow you time to become more comfortable with me as we agreed. However, I think it best I stay in here with you tonight. I don't know about you, but as much as I love my friends, I would like to keep our private business between us. If we kept to our separate rooms on our wedding night, I think it would raise questions they are too tactless not to ask."

He was right. Of course everyone would think it odd if they did not spend the night together, even if it was a marriage of convenience, and she did not wish to deal with questions. While she thought their agreement to be imminently sensible, it was between the two of them and should remain that way, as their intimate business was no one else's. While she should have felt uncomfortable sharing a bed with him having known him for such a short time, she realized with a start that he no longer felt like a stranger. She trusted him.

"All right," she agreed. "I suppose that does make sense. I'll take the right side of the bed."

They made their way over to the bed after he banked the fire, and she felt shy as she removed her wrapper, leaving her in only a thin night rail. She quickly climbed under the covers for extra protection, but Henry politely averted his gaze as he removed his own outer layer. He snuffed out the candle on the bedside table, leaving only the dim glow of the fire lighting the room, and slid in the bed beside her.

Turning his body toward hers, he settled onto his side with his head cradled in the pillow and looked directly at her. "I hope you enjoyed today. I don't know anything about your previous wedding, but from what you've told me about the marriage, I can't imagine there was much to the ceremony."

"No, it was a rather somber affair, I'm afraid. Today was a much lovelier experience. Especially as I knew whom I was marrying beforehand." She made her statement lightly, trying to mask her sorrow and not let him see how much she was still affected by how her first marriage had been arranged. Grace could see from his furrowed brow that he was not fooled. "I hope you don't mind that it was so understated. Moira wanted to make it a much grander affair, and as you are a duke it may have been warranted. But my own desire was to keep the group small and the ceremony simple."

"I thought it was perfect. I would not have wanted a large affair with people I don't really care about in attendance only for the sake of appearances. I was very happy with our small but merry group. The only person who I may have also wanted there was my Aunt Hester, but she is with friends for an extended stay now that her period of mourning is over. I wrote to her of the wedding, but she could not be here in time."

"Tell me more about your aunt. She is the dowager duchess, is she not? Will she reside at the manor with us?"

"She will be away for a while," he answered. "I think she needs some space and time to grieve her son. But she will live at the Manor for a bit when she returns, as I have much to learn from her. I want to honor our family legacy and retain some of the traditions of the dukedom, and she can teach me that. Eventually, she will move to the dower house on the grounds of the estate, but I would like her guidance first."

"Are you close with her?" Grace was curious how this woman might fit into their lives as Henry's closest remaining relative. She desperately hoped they would get along as she had firsthand experience at how difficult it could be when relatives residing in the same space did not get on well. Knowing this woman had been in charge of the manor for many years made her nervous, but she reminded herself that Henry had agreed she would be in charge of running the household.

"Yes and no," he answered. "I saw her once or twice a year as I was growing up when we would all gather at the manor for family holidays. And I spent a few summers with her and my grandparents before I went to school. She and my uncle lived at the manor as he was the heir and learning to manage the estate from my grandfather. I always liked her, she was kind to me, but she takes family tradition very seriously." He became quiet as he thought about his family, many of them now deceased. "It wasn't until she lost her child and I inherited the title that we reconnected at Highland Manor. I really had not seen her much for several years between university and my time away with the army. Even when I returned to England, I rarely left London as my work with the war department kept me bound there." He had a faraway look in his eyes as he recalled his past. "She hardly ever left Somerset, so our paths rarely crossed. We became comfortable around one another once I returned to the manor, but she was quite consumed in her grief."

"I look forward to the day she joins us," Grace said. "I hope spending time in a new setting with friends, away from her grief and memories of your cousin, might be healing for her," Grace said, smiling at him, her eyes growing heavy as the warmth of the bed seeped into her. She began to relax more fully, closing her eyes and her body turning towards Henry's, but could feel the weight of his gaze on her, preventing her from drifting to sleep. "What is it?" she asked, re-opening an eye. "I can feel you looking at me."

"You look so beautiful and peaceful resting in the firelight, I can't help but admire you." He reached out a hand and gently twirled a lock of her hair around his fingers. "I've not seen your hair down before, it's lovely. With the remaining glow from the fire, it looks like spun gold." He spoke quietly, almost reverently. She was not sure what to say, so she continued to look at him while he ran his fingers through her hair. "It is our wedding day, and I promise I will honor our agreement, but do you think you might be willing to give me a goodnight kiss?"

The request made Grace catch her breath. She enjoyed their last kisses, the one by the roses after agreeing to marry, and their kiss after being wed this morning. He had been gentle about it, gathering her close after the Vicar had pronounced them husband and wife, and placing a soft, chaste kiss to her lips. The look of ardor in his eyes as he made his request now, however, made her believe this kiss would be closer to the more passionate kiss they had shared the first time. desire spread through her body as she thought about the possibility, and with the knowledge that she was now his wife, why not allow him another such liberty?

Not breaking from his gaze, she almost imperceptibly nodded her head. He slowly lifted the hand that had been buried in her hair and laid it on her cheek. Angling his body up from the mattress, he spanned the gap that lay between them and closed his lips over her own. Her body awakened at his touch, and she unconsciously moved closer to him. Her response seemed to be the signal he was waiting for as permission for more, and he wrapped his arm around her, pulling her closer until their bodies were aligned and flush against each other. She stiffened for a moment when his arousal brushed against her thigh, but as he was not pressing for anything more than a kiss, she relaxed back into his embrace.

His caress was drugging and lulled her into a dreamlike state. Before she knew what she was doing, she opened her mouth to him in a desire to feel closer and he deepened the kiss. But after a minute, respectful of the boundary that had been set, he pulled back and kissed her forehead, ending the encounter before it could become too heated.

Even though the kiss had ended, Henry did not

release her and kept Grace in his arms, soothingly running his fingers though her hair as they both took a moment to calm their breathing and heart rates to return to normal. "Goodnight, wife," he whispered. "Get some sleep, we have a long ride ahead of us tomorrow."

Cradled next to him, head against his chest and feeling safe for the first time in a long while, she closed her eyes and drifted off to sleep.

CHAPTER 24

Henry awoke the next morning and decided that there was no better feeling in the world than waking up with his wife in his arms. While he had never intended to leave Moira's house party with a wife, he was glad he had not waited to make her his once the idea had been planted.

Waking before her, he was not unhappy to have a few minutes to study her more closely. In sleep, she looked truly at ease for the first time since he had first encountered her with Thomas in the library. Grace carried so many worries, that beautiful as she was, the tension around her eyes was usually clearly visible. But now, still unconscious to the world and its burdens, she looked utterly peaceful and not a wrinkle of concern could be found on her brow.

It was amazing how precious she had become to him in a week's time. But even in that small window, he felt like he understood what motivated her fears to a certain degree. He was honored that after all she had been through, she was choosing to subvert those fears and trust him with her future happiness. He would do everything in his power to make sure she felt appreciated and cared for every day for the rest of her life, deserving nothing less.

Possessing such a gentle and loving spirit, Henry could see how it had been easily crushed when her father died, leaving her unprotected and without affection. He wanted to provide her a safe environment where her true nature, stifled for self-preservation, could bloom once again.

Watching her, he had to suppress a laugh when she shifted slightly, causing a piece of her hair to fall across her face and tickle her nose. Adorably, her nose scrunched at the sensation, much as it had with dust in the library. At remembering such a small detail, Henry was struck with the reality that though neither of them had married for love, he could in fact very easily fall for her. Stunned by the realization, he continued to stare at her without really seeing her as she came fully awake. She stretched in his arms, still only partially awake, and it must have been at that moment she realized she was in fact still nestled next to his side. The next moment she snapped to full alertness and stiffened next to him, blushing at the realization that she was still in his arms.

"Good morning, wife," he said, grinning at her.

"Good morning," she replied. "I hope I didn't crowd you last night, I didn't mean to fall asleep on you."

"You didn't. Besides, I like waking up with you next to me." He felt it was a victory when she did not attempt to move away, allowing him to keep his arm lightly around her. "I should probably return to my own room and allow you to get ready for breakfast. We'll want a hearty meal, as it's going to be a long day of travel. I'm sorry you will have to suffer through it in order to see your new home."

"I will be alright. The fact that I don't have to return to London or my relatives, makes the time on the road worth it," she said with a smile.

Though it was painful to leave her when he wanted to stay next to her warmth, and see if she might allow another kiss, he pulled himself from the bed. A moment later, as he was tightening the sash of his robe, a sharp knock sounded on the door and a maid entered the room, not waiting for admission.

"I'm here to assist you with your morning toilette, Your Grace," the maid said, smirking knowingly at the sight of Grace still lying in the bed.

Clutching the bed covers to her though she was covered by her night rail, Grace blushed furiously at the intimation of marital relations even though such relations had not actually occurred last night. She managed to compose herself before realizing how the maid addressed her. "Oh goodness, I do believe that's the first time I've been called 'Your Grace.' I shall have to get used to that," she said.

"You will have plenty of time to, as it will be your proper address from here forward," Henry said. "I'll leave you now to get ready and will see you again in the breakfast room." He took her hand and kissed it

ANDIE JAMES

before departing, and the blush that clung to her cheeks deepened.

The journey to reach Highland Manor took two long days of travel. It was exhausting even to Henry, and he was used to uncomfortable travel from his years following the army across the continent. Grace obviously felt the effects of the many hours on bumpy road, but she bore it without complaint. The night before when they had stopped at a comfortable Inn he was familiar with in Wiltshire, she had been so exhausted she went straight to her room without even taking supper. Concerned for her, he had a large breakfast delivered to her room in the morning so she would be fortified for the remaining leg of the journey. Joining her, he wanted see if she was well himself, rather than trusting the opinion of the maid who was accompanying them to the manor.

"Come in," she called when he knocked on the door. Upon entering, he was relieved to see she was up and about with color in her cheeks. Grace looked well rested and was sitting at the table, about to tuck into breakfast.

"I'm glad to see you have an appetite this morning. I was worried when you bypassed your evening meal," Henry said.

"Thank you for sending this up," Grace said with a smile. "I am rather ravenous this morning after skipping dinner, but I'm afraid I was too tired to do anything other than fall into bed last night. Will you join me for breakfast?" Grateful she did seem well after a full night's sleep, he pulled up a chair as she poured him a cup of coffee. "Do you take cream or sugar?" she asked. "Goodness, I suppose I need to learn such things." Watching, she noted he picked up the cup unaltered before taking a drink. "Black then, I will remember that for next time."

They ate together in an easy silence and Grace began to ask Henry more questions regarding his preferences. "Do you have a favorite food or meal?"

"I can't say I'm all that picky when it comes to what I eat. After taking whatever is offered for so many years in the army, I've never given much thought to my meals as long as they were routinely provided."

Dreamily, she said, "That is a shame. I find food one of the pleasures of life. Please let me know if there is something you particularly like or don't care for once we reach the manor and I'll have the cook start trying new meals out." Henry liked that she took joy in a good meal and made a mental note to take more notice of what he ate himself and if he did in fact like it.

"What should I expect when I reach Highland Manor?" she asked. Henry was delighted to see her plopping another scone on her plate.

"What do you mean? About the landscape or the house?"

"Well yes, those," she said, laughing lightly. "But also the staff. We were married rather quickly, are they even expecting a new mistress of the house to be arriving?"

"I wrote ahead to alert them to my arrival and told them I would be bringing my new wife with me. If Smyth's reaction is anything to go by, I think they will be well pleased to have a new duchess at the helm."

"I hope so, and I also hope your housekeeper will take to me well," she expressed. "The last thing I want to do is shake up a staff that has served a house for a long time, but I also know that it is common for a new mistress to let a few members of staff go if they do not take on well together or meet her expectations."

"I'm still very much learning the staff myself, but they all seem to know their jobs. It is a place that runs well under the direction Aunt Hester set. I'm sure they will keep things moving along well for you." Henry very much hoped there would be peace in the household, there was nothing worse than tension in a house when there was discord between the staff. He was not worried, however; he knew Grace cared for their well-being, which they would respond well to and would surely ease any discomfort over changes she may wish to make.

Now, hours on the road later after their pleasant breakfast, they were about to cross into the lands of the manor within the heart of Somerset. The carriage wheels skipping along the uneven terrain jostled Grace awake, and Henry watched in amusement as she covered a yawn. Admiring the beautiful countryside with its verdant pastureland and rows of trees chasing the winding waterways that snaked through the land, smiling sheepishly, she asked Henry where they were.

"We are nearly home. We've just passed into manor

lands and should arrive at the house in about half an hour's time." Henry answered.

Grace hummed in approval while taking in the view and clasping her neck, turned her head to the side in an attempt to loosen the stiff muscles.

"Is your neck sore?" he asked in sympathy. "I'm sorry it has been such a long journey."

"It could be worse," she responded. "I'm just glad I've not had another megrim take hold, as travel can induce them."

"Would you like me to rub your neck for you? I'd be more than happy to. It might help ease some of the tension and keep the headaches at bay." He was eager to offer the service as it meant he would be able to get his hands on her soft skin again.

Grace looked surprised at his offer, but agreed to the ministrations saying, "I don't think anyone has offered to do that for me since I was a young lady at my father's house. Are you sure you won't mind?" she asked, wishing to confirm the offer.

"I won't mind at all," he said, scooting closer behind her. "Turn your back to me." He gently brushed aside the soft hairs that had escaped her chignon before pressing his thumb into a knot he found there. Grace closed her eyes and sighed, dropping her forehead, allowing him more access to her neck. "You feel wonderful, and you smell lovely," he murmured, lost in the sensation of her. Her skin was smooth and warm, and he wanted to spend forever caressing it and helping her feel better. After several minutes attention, some of the knots began to loosen, and Henry saw the tension in her shoulders ease, dropping away from her ears. He slowed his touch, feeling her relax back into his chest, and he pulled his arms around her. Neither spoke as they enjoyed the quiet moment, watching the landscape pass in front of them.

As they drew closer to the house, Henry pointed out the tenant farms, the mill, and a few greenhouses along with other landmarks. Finally, they turned down the drive, and the house became visible. It was a large home, but not ostentatious. He observed Grace as she took everything in and hoped she would feel at home here, noticing in particular when she perked up at seeing the well-kept gardens. Within a moment, they pulled to a stop in front of the house.

With the staff awaiting their arrival, a footman Henry didn't recognize rushed forward as soon as the carriage ceased to move and opened the door to assist the new duchess. Henry laughed at the young lad's eagerness and the way he blushed upon seeing Grace.

"Your Grace, we are so glad to welcome you," he said with a bow as he took her hand to help her down the steps.

"Thank you," she said with a smile, looking at the footman directly.

Henry had to keep himself from laughing as he knew this young footman would be charmed just as quickly as Hudson had been at Geffen House. Grace took Henry's arm after he exited the carriage, and they walked toward the manor to greet the staff. Standish, the butler for the past fifteen years at the manor and in service there even longer, stepped forward.

"Your Graces," he said with a bow. "On behalf of the staff, I would like to welcome you home and to congratulate you on your marriage."

"Thank you, Standish," Henry replied with a nod. Looking up so that he could address the staff as a whole, Henry said, "I would like to present to you Her Grace, Grace Ellison, the new Duchess of Carrington." The staff smiled and looked at Grace with curiosity while she predictably blushed and nodded in greeting.

"I just now realized how ridiculous my name sounds next to the honorific," she whispered to Henry. "The double Grace is a bit much."

Henry let out a small snort at her wry observation, and he saw several of the staff members noticing the easy way they interacted, and smiling in approval.

At Standish's beckoning, Mrs. Green, their house-keeper, stepped forward. Standish introduced her along with their cook and under butler, before turning things over to the housekeeper. "It is a pleasure to meet you, Your Grace," she offered. After quickly intro-ducing the remaining members of the staff, she dismissed them back to their work and led Henry and Grace into the house.

Turning back toward Grace, the housekeeper immediately endeared herself to her new mistress when she said, "I imagine after the journey you would like a quiet evening to rest, so we can save the house tour for tomorrow. For tonight, we have prepared baths for you in each of your rooms, and I will have some supper sent up shortly. Standish will arrange for the footmen to bring up your trunks."

Smiling in gratitude at Mrs. Green's thoughtfulness, "That sounds lovely," Grace said in relief. "I find I'm rather worn out after two days on the road. A quiet evening and bath sound like the height of luxury at the moment."

Mrs. Green led them both upstairs and showed them to the Duchess's suite of rooms. "I hope everything is to your liking, but we can change anything to make you more comfortable."

"Thank you, I'm sure you have thought of everything I could need for now. I look forward to getting to know you more tomorrow and seeing the house." Grace smiled at her, and the housekeeper left looking pleased. As Mrs. Green exited, the footman who had assisted Grace earlier appeared with her luggage. She thanked him as he deposited the trunk, and he gave a shy smile before scampering out of the room.

As the door clicked shut behind him, Henry let out a long sigh. He was happy to have a moment alone with Grace after the hustle and bustle of the last few days—staff and service people with them at every turn. "How are you feeling?" he asked her as he helped remove her wrap.

"I'm glad that's over," she admitted. "I'm not sure why, but I was quite nervous to meet the staff for the first time. Perhaps because I feel like an imposter only playing the part of duchess." She sagged into one of the chairs in front of the fire.

"You very much belong here," he said, "and I can tell many of them are already enraptured by you." She sent him a look of disbelief, but he would not have it. "I promise you are worthy of being a duchess," he said as he crouched before her, taking her hands in his. "I've seen how strong you are, even if you doubt yourself. I know you will soon master this new position."

Grace leaned into him and rested her forehead against his, seeking comfort. "Thank you," she whispered.

Henry sat there unmoving, soaking in the peace of being able to sit still and connected with her in this moment. "I will leave you to your bath," he finally said, rising but not releasing her hand. "Would you like to dine on your own, or should I join you here in about an hour?"

"I would like it if you joined me," she replied. "In unfamiliar surroundings, as nice as they are, it would be nice to not feel so alone."

"I would not think to leave you alone unless you wished it. I will see you in an hour then," he said, leaving her to see to his own bath and wash off the weariness of travel.

Feeling refreshed, he returned to her room at the designated time, eager to spend more time with Grace, and knocked on the door. When there was no answer, he knocked again. Hearing no movement in the room, he grew concerned. Calling out her name as he knocked a third time, he opened the door and saw that she was curled up on the bed, fast asleep. With a smile, he tiptoed out of the room.

CHAPTER 25

Grace's first full day at Highland Manor certainly kept her busy. It started off bright and early at breakfast, as she was famished. She felt bad at falling asleep before dining with Henry last night, tiredness had overtaken her for the second night in a row, causing her hunger this morning. Entering the small breakfast parlor at a footman's direction, she was happy to see Henry was already there, immersed in a paper.

Looking up, he greeted her with a smile. "Good morning, wife," he said in the same way he had the first morning they had spent together. "I hope you were able to rest well." He set aside his paper to give her his attention.

"I did, thank you. I'm so sorry that I fell asleep before we could share dinner, I hope you did not have to eat alone."

"Please don't worry yourself over it. Smyth and I ate in my room after he finished unpacking from the trip.

And I was glad you were able to get the sleep you so obviously needed."

She noticed a silver pot full of coffee already in front of him, and she could smell delicious things coming from the sideboard.

"Would you like me to make you a plate?" he offered.

"Oh, no, please don't get up. I can make one for myself," Grace said, picking up a plate from the place setting already laid out on the table. Wandering over to where the buffet was spread, she was astounded by the sheer amount of prepared food before her. There were both scrambled and poached eggs, rashers of bacon, two different kinds of sausage, kippers, porridge, fruit, and a mound of pastries alongside a rack of toast. As she was trying to take it all in, a footman entered the room carrying yet another dish. As soon as he had set it down, he bowed toward her.

"Good morning, Your Grace. Can I get you anything else from the kitchen? What do you prefer to drink in the morning?"

"I certainly don't think we will need any more food, but if you could bring me a pot of tea, it would be most welcome." Before she could ask his name, he bowed again and swiftly left the room. Returning to the buffet, she plated a variety of offerings and joined Henry at the table. "Do you know if a buffet is offered every morning?" she asked him as she took a bite of her eggs.

"I believe so," he answered. Pausing to think, he added, "I'm pretty sure it has been that way as long as I can remember. Why, is it not to your liking?"

"Oh, no, I have no problem with it. Everything looks and tastes delicious . . . It just seems like an awful lot of food to prepare for just the two of us. Do you know if anyone else will eat any of this spread?"

"I'm not sure, but I appreciate that you are conscious of waste," he replied. "You are welcome to change it for the future if you like. You can manage things however you think best."

Henry gave her such an encouraging smile she almost didn't know how to react, still adjusting to having someone around who thought her capable. It warmed her to feel his support. "I'll ask the cook and Mrs. Green about it later. I don't want to make any moves before I have all the information."

After finishing breakfast, Grace left Henry to a meeting with his land manager, catching up on what had happened in his absence, and she wandered downstairs to find Mrs. Green. Passing the kitchen on the way to the housekeeper's office, she stopped to greet the cook, a young woman named Mrs. Nelsen.

"Good morning, Your Grace," the cook greeted her, bowing her head before resuming her stirring. "I hope the breakfast was to your liking." Overhearing the greeting, Mrs. Green stepped out of her office and joined them in the kitchen.

"Everything was delicious," Grace said, "but I did have a question for you regarding the meal."

"Oh, was something the matter, Your Grace?" Mrs. Nelsen looked concerned, and Mrs. Green turned toward her in curiosity.

"No, nothing was the matter," she assured the two

women. "I was simply wondering if such a lavish buffet was always presented, even when there are no guests at home. It seems like a lot of food for only His Grace and I, and I don't want the food to go to waste. Do the staff partake in any of the food as well?"

"Oh," Mrs. Nelsen replied again, seemingly taken aback by the question. "We've always done a buffet regardless of how many people are at home," she said. "No, none of the staff eat the food. We have our morning meal prior to preparing breakfast for you and His Grace, as we are up hours earlier."

"What about luncheon, are you able to repurpose any of the food for either the staff or His Grace?"

"Some of it won't keep," Mrs. Green spoke up, "but Mrs. Nelson is good at reusing what she can, where appropriate."

"I see," Grace said. "Mrs. Nelsen, would it be more work for you or your staff if you were to make individual plates of food for His Grace and I, rather than preparing a buffet? I'd like to cut down on the food waste as well as be more economical, but only if it will not cause you more work."

"Lord, that's kind of you, Your Grace," the cook said, wide-eyed. "While more food would need to go into the luncheon prepared for staff, it would not be more work . . . In fact, it might be easier, as I would not be forced to be as creative with leftovers. The staff would appreciate having more fresh food as well, and preparing less food in the morning for you and His Grace would reduce our workload."

"Excellent," Grace said, smiling at the two women.

"If you both are amenable to it, I think it would be wonderful if only two plates were prepared in the morning for His Grace and I, and feel free to make anything you would like for the staff luncheon moving forward."

Mrs. Nelsen smiled in appreciation, and Mrs. Green noted that it would lead to savings on the larder bill. Grace encouraged Mrs. Nelsen to be creative and surprise her with what she decided to make based on what was seasonal and abundant. Leaving the kitchen, Grace followed Mrs. Green to see the rest of the manor, feeling accomplished in her small victory.

"That was very bold of you," Mrs. Green said as they made their way back up to the main floor. It was said in a kind tone, but Grace felt a twinge of insecurity creep in at her comment.

"What do you mean?" she asked tentatively. "Do you not approve? Should I not make changes so fast?"

"I do approve. I just meant that change has come slowly here in the past." Seeing Grace's look of concern, she was quick to add, "It was a swift decision, yes, but not an uninformed one. You asked all the right questions before you decided to make a change. That's all we can ask for, and it leads to happy staff members." Smiling at Grace, she offered a final commendation. "Well done, Your Grace," she said.

The rest of the day passed in a blur, and before Grace knew it, it was time for her first dinner at the manor. It had turned into a wet night and she listened to the rain tapping against her window as a summer storm was unleashing after quickly mounting that afternoon. She sat at the vanity watching her new lady's maid, Lucy, bustle about the room and pick out items for a suitable dinner dress. Seeing her struggle, Grace apologized for the state of her wardrobe.

She had already known her apparel was lacking but trying to make herself presentable as a duchess made it clear that refurbishing her wardrobe needed to move to the top of her priority list. Her life in Yorkshire had been relatively isolated and the need for formal wear almost nonexistent. Now, her nicer gowns were horribly outdated and came from the time she had been preparing for her coming-out seven years before. Grace had stretched her wardrobe as far as it would go at the house party, updating them herself as much as possible with only passible dressmaking skills, and grateful that her size had not changed dramatically in the intervening years.

Thankfully, Grace had nothing but time to fill while Countess of Camden and decorated many of her simpler gowns with flowery embroidery. But it was clear as she attempted to dress for dinner that what had looked nice in Yorkshire now looked rather shabby in comparison to the well-appointed house around her. While she was not a vain woman, the drapes in her room were made of nicer material than most of her gowns, and she was self-conscious about going down to dinner.

"Don't you fret, Your Grace," Lucy said, now

arranging her hair. "I've a fine hand with a needle myself, and I'm sure His Grace won't even notice. You know how men are, he'll be too distracted by your pretty face to even notice what you're wearing. That is, until he goes to take it off you later," she said with a wink.

"Lucy!" Grace admonished while turning crimson. "You should not speak of such things. And yes, His Grace is a perfect gentleman and would never comment on my attire even if he did notice." Pulling on her gloves, she was finally ready to head downstairs. "Thank you, Lucy. I appreciate your help. I'll talk with the duke this evening to see about arranging for some new dresses to be made. And I would like you to accompany me when I go to the dressmaker." Grace still had a long way to go to feel confident she was the woman Henry thought her capable of being and looking the part would help her pretend until she was comfortable in her new surroundings.

Grace was relieved at how pleasantly dinner was going, Henry being easy to talk with and the food divine. She had told him about the breakfast changes, and he not only supported her decision but was happy she was already making changes to feel at home. As dessert was served, she tentatively raised the idea of funds, something they had yet to discuss.

"Henry," she said, not looking at him while fiddling with her spoon, running it through the custard at the bottom of the pudding bowl. "I wondered if I might ask you a question regarding how much I am able to spend for the household and other items."

"I'm not entirely sure how much has normally been budgeted for the household as Aunt Hester remained in charge when I took over the title, but I can look in the books and Mrs. Green can cover normal monthly expenses with you," he replied, seemingly unconcerned.

"Yes, she showed me the books today," Grace replied. "Mrs. Green and Standish run a tight ship without skimping on what is needed to live comfortably. I suppose I'm asking more about what I might be allowed to spend on items that are more frivolous and less necessary in nature." She now looked up at him and saw that he seemed puzzled as to what she was really asking. Not surprising as she was being rather vague, finding it hard to gather the courage to plainly ask for what she needed.

"Is there something in particular you need?" he asked. "If you want to redo some of the rooms after seeing them on your tour today, we can discuss a budget. I am more than happy to let you put your own touch on the place."

"No, no, the house is lovely," she said, flustered. "It might be prudent to make some updates in time, but nothing in the manor seems to be a pressing need at the moment. I suppose I'm trying to work my way up to telling you that I should like to update my wardrobe some, if you think it a wise investment." At this she looked down again and felt her telltale blush starting.

"Grace, look at me," he said, reaching across the table for her hand. "I don't want you to ever feel that you cannot ask me for such things. I was remiss in not discussing financial matters with you and not sharing an allowance so you would not feel uneasy asking about such things." She smiled as he continued. "The Dukedom of Carrington is comprised of three working estates, the London house in Mayfair, and a seaside home near Bath. The estates are well run, and I have invested in improvements in farming equipment, so we should soon see a return on investment with higher yields, assuming the weather holds." A flash of lightning lit the room, and they grinned at one another as thunder cracked in the background.

"While I never want to spend outlandishly," he continued, "and it seems neither of us want extravagant lives," she nodded her unspoken agreement as he finished, "we don't need to worry about spending on everyday expenses. And I know what you are going to say, but clothing is something that must be warn daily, so it is a necessity. I should have told you this sooner, and I apologize for not doing so, but I have arranged for a seamstress from a well-known modiste to visit the manor and take your measurements. She should arrive in the next day or two and start work on new dresses and gowns for you."

Stunned, Grace hardly knew what to say. "Thank you, that was very thoughtful. Whenever did you arrange such a thing?"

"I visited the modiste while I was in London preparing for the wedding, and I told the seamstress to spare no expense on a brand-new wardrobe. She will bring with her all the items for which measurements are not needed, such as gloves, stockings, and things—I don't even know what. While she is here you can discuss your needs and she will ship items as she makes them." He looked at her pointedly, waiting for her to protest.

Not one to disappoint, she couldn't help but push back at the generosity. "Henry, it's too much," she said with a sigh. "Yes, I need some new clothing, but an entirely new wardrobe? Lucy and I can alter and fix what I already have if nice trimmings can be acquired."

"Grace, when is the last time you had a new dress?" he asked her pointedly.

"I suppose about two and a half years ago. . ."

"And when was the last time you had a new evening gown?"

"Seven years ago . . . in preparation for my debut," Grace said, blushing.

"Then do you not believe you deserve something new? Please let me take care of you as you deserve."

Grace nodded, though a small part of her still wanted to protest. "Thank you, Henry. I truly am grateful. Please be patient with me. I'm still adjusting to having someone care about my wellbeing. It is a jarring, but welcome, change."

Gazing at her with a soft look in his stunning gray eyes, he said, "I will give you as much time as you need, but I will also continue to give you what you deserve, so be prepared."

CHAPTER 26

It was the unusual sound of breaking glass the jolted Henry awake more than the crash of thunder which accompanied it. The startled shriek that emitted from the direction of Grace's bedroom was what had him on his feet and rushing toward her before he was even fully cognizant, wrenching open the connecting door.

"Stop!" Grace cried out from her bed. "There is broken glass on the floor, you'll cut your feet."

Just then, a footman on night duty burst in from the hallway. "What's wrong, Your Grace?" he spluttered, looking around the room, holding a candle aloft.

Assessing the situation from his place in the door-frame, Henry grasped what had happened. "Everyone stay where you are," Henry ordered, eyeing a large tree branch that had crashed through the window as the storm intensified, more servants appearing as he spoke. "Grace, are you alright?" When she nodded her head, seeing there was no immediate emergency, he took charge. "Grace, don't move from the bed, I'll be right back for you." Gesturing toward the footmen just inside the doorframe, he said, "You two, go and get something to clean up the glass and water and find something to board up the window." He left to put on shoes and don his dressing gown before returning to the room.

Picking his way across the floor, he was relieved to see that the bed avoided much of the damage positioned as it was in the room. But with the window shattered and open to the elements, the room had grown cold, and rain was blowing in almost horizontally, soaking the quilt at the foot of the bed. Pulling the damp covers back, he flinched at the tinkling of glass as small shards fell to the floor. "Did any of the glass hit you?" he asked Grace as he examined her in the dim light of the mostly extinguished fire. Running his hands over her arms, he felt for cuts.

"I think a small piece cut my cheek," she replied, raising a hand to her face, and wincing as she felt her cheekbone. Pushing her hair back so he could see the side of her face, he cursed under his breath when he saw a thin line of blood.

"Come on, let's get you out of here." Before she could protest, he swept her up in his arms and carried her into his bedchamber. Setting her down on the bed, he grabbed a blanket and wrapped it around her shaking shoulders before lighting a brace of candles.

"I'm well, really," she tried to reassure him. "I don't think I'm cut anywhere else and I'm hardly even damp."

He ran his hand through her hair and cradled her face, guiding her chin up to the light so he could better assess the cut. "It doesn't look deep, but we'll need to clean it out. I'll have Lucy grab you a new night rail and some antiseptic to clean the wound." His heart was racing, and he took a moment for a deep breath to calm his nerves, as this was the first chance he'd had in the minutes since he first sprang from bed to slow down. Henry was always calm during a crisis, but no longer needing to manage the situation, the fear he had felt thinking something had happened to Grace was catching up with his body. His arms and hands felt fluttery, and he thought his knees might give out from beneath him.

"Henry, sit down," Grace said, pulling his arm until he sank onto the bed beside her. "You're trembling."

Taking in another deep breath, he replied, "You are too. It's the shock, it'll pass in a moment." Grace soothingly stroked his back as his breathing returned to normal. "You scared the life out of me," he finally said. "I wasn't sure if you were injured."

"Only superficially," she said reassuringly, "and I believe it was the tree that scared you, not I." The last was said with a slight smirk.

"Semantics," he grunted. "I'm just glad it wasn't worse. Are you sure you're alright?"

"A little shaken," she admitted, "but I promise I'm fine," she added, smiling. She gently brushed his hair off his forehead and said, "At the moment I'm more worried about you. I've never seen you out of sorts. But I must say, the way you did not hesitate to take action was quite compelling." She lowered her eyes and blushed. He started to feel warm and slightly aroused and was leaning in to kiss her before hearing a knock from across the room.

Clearing his throat while averting his eyes, Standish informed them, "The room has been cleared, Your Graces. We've covered the window and cleaned the room of glass. It might be best for the duchess to stay elsewhere until the window has been replaced, at least for tonight."

Having pulled away from Grace, Henry composed himself and answered. "Thank you, Standish, for the quick work. Her Grace can stay here with me. Will you please send Lucy in? You can return to bed and let the rest of the staff retire as well."

"Very good, Your Grace. Have a good evening," Standish said with a bow before exiting. Lucy appeared in what felt like seconds, and Henry sent her for supplies to tend to Grace. Within minutes her cut had been tended and she was warmly ensconced in new night clothes.

"Thank you, Lucy," Grace told the maid. "I appreciate your ministrations. Go get some sleep."

"I'm glad you are all right, Your Grace," Lucy offered with a shy smile before leaving the two of them alone after a hectic half an hour.

Grace looked worn-out as the final traces of adrenaline left her system, and all Henry wanted to do was hold her. "Let's go to bed," he suggested and moved to blow out the candles. He heard the rustle of Grace pulling back the covers and cautiously made his way to the other side of the bed, feeling his way in the dark. Removing his dressing gown, he slipped under the covers and joined her in the bed. He reached for her, and she did not resist, obviously needing some comfort after the unexpected events of the last hour.

When her head hit his bare shoulder, she pulled back in shock from feeling his skin. "You're not clothed!"

He chuckled at her reaction, utterly charmed by her primness. "I'm not naked, I promise. I just don't like to feel restricted by a shirt when I sleep. Did you not notice I was only wearing trousers when I first entered your room?"

"I guess now that you mention it, I can only picture you in a loose set of pants. . . I guess I was too distracted by everything else for it to sink in."

"If you're bothered by it, I'm happy to put on a shirt," he offered.

"No, I want to you to be comfortable. This is your room and your bed. I'm the one intruding on your normal sleeping arrangements, please don't feel like you need to change to accommodate me." She tentatively settled down next to him, and he wrapped an arm around her back, drawing her in close.

"I would be happy for you to interrupt my sleeping habits anytime," he whispered in her ear. "I like having you beside me." He felt a shiver run through her body at his words, followed by her delicate touch as she placed a palm against his bare chest. He kissed the top of her head as she nestled into the space where his shoulder met his neck, and after a few minutes, they both fell back to sleep.

CHAPTER 27

Grace woke the next morning cocooned in warmth. It took her a moment to notice that, rather than a pillow, her cheek was resting on warm, firm skin. Remembering the events of the evening before, she recalled where she was. Though she could be offended by the position she was in due to the agreement with Henry, allowing her space and time before engaging in the physical nature of marriage, she chose to ignore what she ought to feel. Instead, she decided there was nothing wrong with indulging in the comfort her husband's naked chest was currently providing her.

It wasn't but a moment later that Henry began to stir beneath her. "Mmmhh, good morning, wife," he mumbled into her hair before stretching his arms, accentuating his toned chest. She couldn't help but stare.

He was in healthy shape, likely from his years spent in the army, and Grace could see the muscles ripple as he rolled his shoulders back, shaking off the fog of sleep. A light dusting of dark brown hair covered his pectorals, only highlighting his manliness. Gazing upon him made her feel warm, and she looked away before her blush could betray her.

"It's alright, Grace. You can look at me."

His voice came from behind her as she curled into herself, fighting off new ideas and sensations from the sight of him. Calling upon her bravery, knowing she would not be able to avoid him forever, she rolled back to face him.

"Your so skittish with me, do I make you uncomfortable?" he asked with a creased brow, showing his concern.

"No, I actually feel quite comfortable with you, I'm just not used to being so intimately close with a man." He still looked puzzled, no doubt due to the fact that she was a widow and no stranger to sharing her body. "I never saw my previous husband naked," she said, feeling she needed to offer him more and surprised that she actually wanted to. "He always kept his sleep shirt or dressing gown on whenever he would come to me."

"You did not share a bed?" he asked as he brushed his fingers across the cut on her cheek. She shook her head. "That is a shame," he said, leaning in closer to her, "because it is wonderful to wake up next to the person you desire."

He breathed across her lips, and she shuddered at the sensation, knowing he was about to kiss her. He leaned a fraction of an inch further, and when she did not pull back, proceeded to press his lips against hers. He was not aggressive, but he also did not go in slowly. Boldly using sustained pressure before he slid his tongue across her bottom lip asking her for access, she gasped, opening her mouth. He gently entered her mouth and proceeded to reduce her to bone-lessness as he fed off her with his kisses for several minutes like he was starving for her.

She had become so enthralled that it took her a moment to notice his hand sliding up the outside of her thigh where her night rail had become bunched beneath the twisted covers. The feel of his hand on her skin rising even higher set her ablaze as he left a trail of heat everywhere he touched. She was sure it would leave a permanent burn, marking her forever. His hand finally came to rest at her hip, almost to the curve of her waist, and she could feel his fingers graze the top of her buttocks.

He finally pulled away from her mouth, but before she could catch her breath, his lips had moved down her jaw to her neck, and continued to move down, sliding across her collarbone. When he reached the edge of her night rail that rested at the top swell of her bosom, he edged his face lower and used the tip of his nose to nuzzle her breast through the material. The sensation overwhelmed her, and her body started to feel restless, writhing of its own accord. When she arched her back and her pelvis surged into his hard stomach, she came back to herself with a start.

Gasping, she forced her eyes open and shoved herself out of his arms. "I can't," she gasped, covering her eyes with her hands. "I'm so sorry, I can't."

Henry rolled away from her onto his back. He lay there for a moment, catching his breath, and she watched as he scrubbed a hand over his face.

"I'm sorry if you're upset with me," she whispered.

"I'm not upset with you," he said, looking at her. "I promise. I'm upset with myself for moving so quickly. I didn't mean to push you."

"You did nothing wrong," she cried, "it was me. I behaved like an utter wanton. I don't know what came over me, I'm so sorry!" she practically wailed, hiding her face in the pillow in mortification.

"I don't understand," she heard him say. He tentatively placed a hand on her shoulder. "Do you think the way you responded to me was inappropriate?"

Turning her head to peer at him with one eye, she asked, "Do you not think so?"

"No, I don't," he said firmly. "I think you were a woman indulging her desires." He looked at her intently for a moment before gently asking, "Grace, when I first kissed you, you said that your late husband had never kissed you, and this morning you told me you had never seen him naked. Did you not feel passion in your first marriage?"

Sitting up a bit, Grace took a deep breath. "You already know that my marriage was not an entirely happy situation." He nodded at her but remained quiet, allowing her to speak. "While my husband and I were married for six years before he died, I can count on two hands the number of times he came to my bed." The heat of her ever-present blush warmed her cheeks at her admission, and she stared at her lap, playing with the sheet while continuing her tale. She knew she owed him more of an explanation for their relationship to progress, but she didn't feel like she could share everything just yet.

"He was not rough with me, nor did he hurt me, but it was never a pleasant experience. He simply got down to business with nothing to prepare me for what was to come." Henry took her hand without interrupting her, seeming to realize she needed to share her story in her own time. "His infrequent visits didn't make sense, as he had told my cousin he was seeking a wife because he wanted an heir. There was one point where I thought I may have conceived, but if I did, it did not take and the baby never grew." She paused for a minute, mourning the children she never had. "I always felt like something must be wrong with me, but I didn't know what to do . . ." She took a minute to remind herself she now knew that not to be true, but that was a part of the story she was not yet ready to share, no matter how much she trusted Henry. "I'm sorry I don't know what to expect, I'm sure I must be a disappointment to you."

Henry kissed the top of her head, then said, "I want you to listen to what I have to say, and to really hear me. There is nothing wrong with you. You are completely lovable and desirable. Which is a problem because I am trying to be a gentleman when all I want to do is put my hands on you." Hearing how much he desired her, she pressed her face into his chest, glad he could not see it as it reddened, and he tightened his hold on her.

"You are not wanton for following the desires of your body. It is not wrong to feel pleasure. I promise there is so much more to lovemaking than what you have experienced." He kissed her head again and rubbed circles on her back before asking, "Is that why you asked to wait to make consummate our marriage? Because you thought it would be uncomfortable, or you thought I would be disappointed?"

"Yes," she said into his chest. "I thought maybe some of the uncomfortableness had stemmed from never really knowing him. I thought that if I could learn more of who you were, I might not be so intimidated when it came down to it. I suppose I must seem rather naïve and foolish to you."

"No, you are not, and I promise you can never disappoint me. Don't be scared of the things you feel, they are natural, and you should follow your pleasure. Doing so does not make you wanton, and I will not think less of you for it. The fact that you are so passionate only makes you more attractive and desirable to me. Remember when I told you things mean more when the other person wants it as well?" She nodded into his chest. "The same applies here. Lovemaking is better when both people are fully enjoying themselves. Please don't hold back from me."

Feeling secure enough, she pulled back enough to be able to see his face. "I'll try not to, but just like with

LOST AND FOUND BY THE DUKE

adjusting to my role of duchess, please be patient with me."

"Always," he said, lightly grabbing her chin so she was forced to look him in the eye. "We can go at the pace you feel comfortable with, I won't rush you. Just be open to how you feel."

CHAPTER 28

The next two weeks were busy as Henry and Grace settled into life together at Highland Manor. Most of the staff had immediately taken to Grace just as Henry had predicted, though he heard Standish grumbling about changes from time to time. For his part, Henry either did not notice the changes or thought they were an improvement, and it made him happy to see Grace growing in confidence as she took the reins. At Grace's insistence, he also took her around the estate so she could see the farms and meet the tenants. Every few days she would make her way to another part of the grounds to spend time with the occupants and bring them treats and supplies.

As for the intimate side of their relationship, things had only improved since the talk they had about her previous experience. It had taken two weeks to replace her window, and during that time, Grace remained in his room until the repairs could be completed. They used the time to become more comfortable with each other, and Henry loved nothing more than holding her in his arms. She seemed to fit there perfectly, as if she had always belonged, just as he had felt the very first time he had picked her up at Geffen House. While their explorations of one another had remained relatively tame, being with her was incendiary, and she now felt bold enough to initiate kissing him regularly. Last night, with the window fixed, she had returned to her own bed and he had missed her terribly.

Henry was slowly becoming more comfortable within his own skin and the idea of being a duke. While it had been just over a year, finally settling into the manor without the blanket of shock and grief hanging over it, it was all starting to feel real. Settling into his study, he took up that morning's newspaper to read about the political strife in London. Tensions were mounting between the classes as Reid had predicted, and he feared things might get out of hand if concessions could not be reached in the next Parliamentary session, making his seat in the House of Lords feel even more significant. It was the last major step Henry needed to take in terms of duties of his title, and he keenly felt the responsibility of sitting in that chamber.

A knock sounded on the study door, and he looked up from the paper to see Grace standing in the doorway. "Well, aren't you a beautiful sight," he said, causing her to blush as she smiled at him. "To what do I owe the pleasure of your company?"

"I just wanted to let you know that I'll be in the garden most of the day, should you need me. We're planning and planting for the kitchen garden and preparing for fall produce." He was glad to see that she looked at ease and seemed to enjoy being an active presence in the household. Most of the staff had had taken to her leadership well and were excited about the subtle changes she was making to operations, allowing things to run more smoothly. Standish, always a traditionalist as he had been brought up to run things under the tutelage of his aunt, was having a bit more difficulty adjusting. He seemed to view the changes Grace was implementing as a personal affront, but like the good servant he was, he complied with her requests, though he did so with a stiffness and occasional frown of disapproval.

"Enjoy your time digging in the dirt, my dear," he teased. "I shall miss you while you are away."

"Well, we can't have that. I'll just have to leave you something to remember me by," Grace said as she walked over to him and grasping his face in her delicate hands, placed a sweet kiss on his lips. Henry gave himself over to the kiss and reveled in the new boldness he was seeing come to life in her. "I'll see you later," she said, now shy again, before releasing his face. Watching as she left the room, Henry marveled at his luck.

Stretching to loosen his muscles after being hunched over ledgers for hours, Henry decided to go and find his wife, anxious to see how her project was turning out. Making his way to the back of the house, he was startled to hear raised voices. Henry became even more alarmed when he recognized one of those voices as Grace's. Hurrying forward, he found Grace, Standish, Mrs. Green, and two young men, all in a heated discussion. He recognized one of the men as a gardener and the other was in the livery of a footman.

Not yet able to tell what was going on, he tried to pick up on cues before inserting himself into the situation. Mrs. Green stood off to the side between the young men whose heads were lowered while Standish and Grace were having a heated argument, his face a purple hue as she gesticulated wildly. The footman in particular seemed to be distressed, though not directly involved in the argument. That was strictly being waged between Standish and his wife. While Grace's back was to him, he could tell she was clearly agitated by the ridged stance she held. And used to Standish as a generally placid man, Henry wasn't sure he had ever seen him so animated.

"They cannot remain in employment, it is simply disgraceful," Standish spat.

"And I'm telling you that they should not lose their place over this, they have done nothing wrong" Grace returned forcefully. At Standish's continued blustering, she continued. "Tell me, have they been neglectful in performing their duties? Have you found their work to be subpar? Because if not, then they should not be let go."

Henry had never seen Grace so worked up before, and he wanted to support her if at all possible. "What's going on? Whatever has happened?" he asked as he stepped forward, using the commanding tone of his army years.

"Your Grace," Standish spluttered, "please inform your wife that we have a code of conduct that we expect all staff to follow, otherwise they understand they will be terminated."

Glaring at the butler for insinuating he should tell Grace what to do, Henry turned toward the house-keeper. "Mrs. Green, you seem to have a cool head at the moment, perhaps you can enlighten me to what has happened?"

"Of course, Your Grace," she said while giving a slight bow. "I was not directly involved, but it seems that Standish came across these two young men in an intimate embrace."

"They were kissing in plain sight, it's not right!" Standish exploded.

"I would hardly call their private quarters to be in plain sight, Standish," Grace retorted. "You stumbled upon a private moment when you entered their personal quarters unannounced. Honestly, I would say you were the one who broke rules of conduct by entering their space without permission."

"How and where I found them does not matter," Standish retorted. "What they were doing is still wrong, and they should not be allowed to remain working for this household."

Henry saw the footman flinch out of embarrass-ment while the gardener maintained a blank face,

ANDIE JAMES

trying to seem unaffected by the shouting around them.

"And I'm telling you," Grace said through gritted teeth, "they should not be let go for this. Who have they harmed? No one. As long as they are still able to perform the jobs for which they have been hired, then they shall have a place here. If they continue to keep their private lives private, *as they were*, then no one needs to be bothered and they can go about their work. Love harms no one, and I refuse to terminate them because of it."

"But it's simply not right," Standish stubbornly continued. Turning toward Henry, he said, "This never would have been allowed when your aunt was in charge."

Staring the butler down, he said, "That may be, but my aunt is no longer in charge, my wife is. As the duchess, Grace runs this household, and I have the utmost faith and confidence in her. I'm surprised that you would question her directive at all." Standish looked as if Henry had slapped him, shocked not to have the duke's support.

"Come now, let's get back to work," Mrs. Green said, motioning at the young men. Turning, she shuffled the men out of the room and gave a small bow on her way out. "Good afternoon, Your Graces."

Standish still stood dumbfounded. After a moment, he turned toward Henry and bowed as well. "Your Grace," he said, ignoring Grace before turning and walking out of the room. With everyone gone, Grace seemed to wilt as she turned to bury her face against

Henry's chest. He immediately wrapped his arms around her and stroked the back of her head while she composed herself.

Finally, she stepped back and looked up at Henry. "I hate that once again I was not able to stand up for myself—that my own words were not sufficient and I needed you to save me. But nonetheless, I am thankful for your support."

"And you shall always have it," he reassured her. "Do you want to tell me what is really going on? I've never seen you so passionate as you were when defending those boys." This seemed personal, like it meant something to you." He wanted to understand and didn't like that there were still parts of her that he didn't know.

"I promise I'll explain later," she told him. "I think I owe you that. But for now, I need to return to my work. I don't think I can speak about this with objectivity at the moment."

"Of course," Henry said, not wanting to push her when she was still uneasy from the confrontation. Leaning over to kiss the crown of her head, he then released her and watched as she returned to the garden.

CHAPTER 29

As she prepared for bed that evening, Grace knew the time had come to fully explain her past to her husband. The incident this afternoon with Standish and the young men had brought up too many emotions and left her feeling vulnerable. Walking toward the door that connected her bedchamber with Henry's, she knocked.

"Come," he commanded. He looked up from a chair in front of the fire and gave her a warm smile. "I hoped you might join me," he told her, "I missed not having you with me last night." Grace blushed at his words, but she had missed him as well. With the glass in her window replaced, she had returned to her room the evening before as seemed proper. She had not anticipated that she would have grown accustomed sleeping with Henry beside her in such a short amount of time. She had not slept well last night and longed for his arms to be around her again. But first they needed to talk.

"I wanted to talk with you about why I reacted so strongly to Standish this afternoon. I think I need to explain a few things about my previous marriage." Expression serious, Henry nodded, allowing her to speak, but she stood there awkwardly, unsure where to begin.

"It's been a long day," he said, "why don't we get settled in bed and you can tell me when you are more comfortable?" Grace breathed a sigh of relief and pulled back the covers. She nestled into the soft sheets, laid her head on Henry's chest, and took a deep breath before beginning.

"I was upset this afternoon because I feel strongly people should be able to love whomever they want, regardless of circumstances, as long as no one is harmed. Class should not matter, nor if they are male or female." She gauged Henry for a reaction, but he remained relaxed and had not altered his hold on her. She took it as a good sign and continued. "I honestly believe that the world would be a much happier and better place if we did not put so many social barriers around who is or is not an appropriate match, and love was allowed to develop freely." Sitting up, Grace rested against the headboard so she could see Henry's face. He appeared thoughtful and was listening intently. "A few weeks ago, I told you that my husband and I hardly had a physical relationship"—he nodded in acknowledgment— "but I didn't fully explain why, and I never told you the nature of how he died." Henry, while curious, remained silent, allowing her space to tell the story at her own pace.

"I thought there was something wrong with me, that he found me undesirable" she continued, picking at the edge of the bedsheet. "I tried to make myself more amenable, to do small things for him, trying to make him happy. But as time went on, he seemed to withdraw from me even more. He became harsher and seemed to resent me. I couldn't understand it." The frustration she had felt for so long was rippling just beneath the surface in the retelling, but she shook the feeling away.

"It wasn't until he died that everything became clear. He was found stabbed inside of a molly-house along with his paramour. It seems that an ex-lover of my husband's partner had burst in on them while they were together and killed them in a jealous rage." She looked at Henry again, and though he looked surprised, she was happy to see no sign of revulsion at her revelation.

"I know I was supposed to be outraged and horrified by the nature of his death, but all I felt was relief. Everything finally made sense—the way he was always drunk when he came to couple with me, why he couldn't look at me when we procreated and would never kiss me, and why he did not want to be around me." She paused to wipe a tear from her cheek, recalling how lonely and confused she had felt. "It turns out, there had been nothing wrong with me, he just couldn't feel attracted to me as a woman. I'm sure his growing anger toward me came from feeling as trapped in our marriage as I did." Henry reached out and took her hand, squeezing it in a show of his support.

"I just wish he would have told me . . ." she continued shakily, reaching the end of her emotional tether. "Maybe if he had trusted me and let me know of his attraction to men, we could have come to an understanding between us . . . managed to live our lives together as companions. I can't even begin to understand the pressure he must have felt and the fear he was living under, I would have happily allowed him to take his pleasure in the way he desired. I wish I could have helped him, been a friend." She looked down at Henry to gage his reaction now that everything was on the table. "Are you disgusted with me?" she asked.

"No, I just feel sad for both of you," he said. "I've also known men who had to hide their desire for other men, and I know it can be difficult to either deny or keep secret such an important part of themselves. I'm sorry for the effect it had on you." Grace's eyes welled at Henry's easy acceptance.

"Come here," he said tenderly as he sat up and opened his arms to her. She leaned into the comfort of his warm body, feeling secure.

"That is why you defended those young men today, because you want them to be able to live freely, as your husband could not?" Henry asked into her temple.

"Yes," Grace agreed. "There is no reason they should be let go simply for being discovered in a private moment. I understand that many people do not accept such attraction and love; I don't resent Standish for feeling that way. But I draw the line at punishing anyone when their actions do no harm and they perform well at their jobs."

"I love that you have such a kind heart, and I agree with you. I want our home to be a place where everyone can live as they are." He pulled her even closer and kissed the crown of her head. "Thank you for sharing everything with me . . . for trusting me. I know that couldn't have been easy."

"I do trust you, Henry," she said, looking up at him, startled to realize just how true that was. Grace recognized she no longer feared that her marriage to him would be anything like her last. He had shown her nothing but support from the very first time she met him. Defending her against Thomas, and again today with Standish, he demonstrated his respect for her authority. Henry allowed her to be herself and appreciated her just as she was. Overcome by her feelings, and realizing just how much she loved him, she reached up and pulled him into a passionate kiss.

Henry returned the kiss eagerly, and soon heat rose up her spine as his body hovered over hers. With her newly discovered feelings of love, she was overwhelmed by the desire to be closer to him. Pulling back from the heated embrace, she looked him in the eyes. "I'm ready, Henry," she said breathlessly.

"You mean . . ." he said, a bit drunk sounding after the kiss. She nodded in affirmation.

"There's nothing I want so much as to feel close to you. It means everything that you have waited for me."

Desire shone from his eyes as he looked at her. "You're sure?" he said, asking again just to be clear what she was consenting to.

"Yes, I trust you," she whispered as he breached the distance between them to kiss her.

Henry was as gentle, patient, and loving with her as Grace had expected. As he continued kissing her, each kiss becoming more insistent with the press of their lips, he slowly undressed her, taking his time to move his lips down her body, making it come alive until she was desperate for more. Following the instincts of her body without the shame and vulnerability she had felt previously, the love and safety she felt when she was with Henry allowed her to drop her inhibitions and give herself over, surrendering to the overwhelming sensations.

When they were finally joined, Grace couldn't remember ever feeling so close or connected to anyone as she felt with Henry in that moment. She had never experienced the marriage bed as pleasurable before, but this was different, this was making love. The sense of pleasure continued to build until a wave of ecstasy crashed over her, leaving her boneless in Henry's arms. Henry shuddered and collapsed next to her, rolling to her side to not crush her, though she welcomed the feel of his weight, like a blanket protecting her.

Collecting her breath and returning to her body, Grace looked at Henry, her husband in all ways now, before resting her head on his shoulder.

"Are you alright?" he asked her, stroking her hair.

"I'm perfect," she answered him. "Thank you for choosing me, Henry."

"Thank you for choosing me back," he said quietly, before kissing the top of her head. Relaxing under his gentle ministrations, Grace found herself slowly drifting into sleep.

CHAPTER 30

Waking early the next morning, Henry buried his nose in Grace's hair and breathed in the sweet, floral scent of roses that would forever remind him of his wife, and his growing love and admiration for her. He felt like he was in a dream and recalled how precious last evening had been. He was glad she had fully opened up about her marriage, and deeply honored that she had trusted him enough to share her body with him. With further insight into her insecurities, the fact she felt enough support from him to stand up for herself yesterday was the best feeling in the world. He loved watching her blossom as her confidence was restored.

He knew Grace would not be whole overnight—It was a process that would take time. She had been so consistently undermined that it would take more than the five months since her husband had died, and the revelation of his attractions, for her to reverse the years of self-doubt she had felt. He vowed to stand by and support her as she continued to rediscover herself, finding joy again.

Thinking about what her trust had allowed to unfold last night, Henry grinned remembering how much he had enjoyed discovering her. He was more than eager to repeat the experience, and he hoped Grace would be as well, but he was willing to be patient as she explored this new aspect of their relationship. While he had been with other women over the years, none of his experiences had equaled the emotional impact he had felt in joining with Grace. Being with her had felt different, and he knew it was due to his deepening affection.

His thoughts were interrupted by a knock on the door. It was much too early for it to be Smyth, causing him concern. Hearing another knock, he climbed out of bed trying not to disturb Grace, pulling on a dressing gown before hurrying to the door.

"Yes?" he said to a footman waiting there, after quietly opening the door.

"I'm sorry to disturb you so early, Your Grace, but an urgent message for you has just been delivered." The footman passed Henry a letter before leaving with a bow. Closing the door and turning toward the window for light, Henry opened the letter.

"What is it?" Grace asked sleepily, the light from the parted drapes stirring her awake.

Henry scanned the contents of the letter and uttered an obscenity under his breath. "There's been a fire at the estate up north. I'll need to ride up there right away and assess the damage." He looked up at her and wanted to curse fate for making him leave her so quickly after reaching a deeper level of their relationship.

Moving to her bedside, he kneeled and cupped Grace's face. "I don't want to leave you, especially not today. How are you feeling after last night?"

She blushed and lowered her eyes. "I am well. I enjoyed our time together," she admitted bashfully. "But don't let me keep you. I can help you get ready to travel."

"I hate to leave you alone after yesterday's tension. Do you feel comfortable with the household staff?" He knew she could stand on her own two feet and did not need him to back her up, but he wanted to make sure she felt able to move forward without him there to support her.

"I'll be fine. The only one who was upset was Standish, and he's too much of a professional to let it hinder is work moving forward." Henry leaned in and kissed her, soft and long, before standing to get ready for his journey.

The next few hours were a whirlwind of preparations before Henry and Smyth set out. Grace and the staff had hurried to get everything he would need together for a trip of undetermined length. Finally, everything loaded into the carriage that would follow him on horseback, departure could no longer be delayed. Grace approached his mount and fed him an apple before scratching the horse's nose.

"Take good care of him for me," she whispered to the horse, who snickered in agreement.

"I'll be fine, I promise," he said, sidling up behind her. "I'll return to you as soon as I can." Turning around and throwing herself into his arms, Grace squeezed him tightly before letting him go. The embrace being much too quick for Henry, he reached out and brought her back against him, pressing a scorching kiss to her lips before loosening his hold. Pulling back and panting, he rested his forehead against hers. "Take care while I'm gone," he said. With a proper goodbye in place, he mounted his horse, and rode down the drive, heart aching at leaving.

A few hours later, Henry pulled off the main road and turned toward the estate where his Aunt Hester was currently staying. Earlier that morning, he had decided he would ask his aunt to return to Highland Manor while he was away to be an extra support and company for Grace. Arriving at the main house, he was anxious to hear what his aunt's thoughts were regarding his marriage.

At the door, once Henry had explained who he was, he was led immediately to a morning room where his aunt was busy composing letters. As he was announced, she looked up in shock.

"Well this is a most welcome surprise," Aunt Hester said at the sight of Henry as she rose to kiss him. "What brings you here? And what on earth were you thinking becoming married so hastily, and without my guidance?"

Henry stood, mouth agape, never anticipating such a response.

"Well? What do you have to say for yourself for

behaving in such a brash manor?" she asked, shaking her head in exasperation. "I assume she's either a title or fortune hunter for everything to have happened so quickly. How were you so foolish as to fall for such a trap? You should know what an attractive target you became when you ascended to the title."

Henry was astounded. "I would think very carefully what you say next about my wife, Aunt Hester," he cautioned her. "Grace is a wonderful woman, and I assure you she did not trap me into anything."

Aunt Hester sniffed, ready to move onto other topics of conversation having said her piece. "Not that it's not wonderful to see you, but what are you doing here so unexpectedly?"

"There's been a fire at the northern estate. I'm on my way there now to look into the damage, but I had thought to stop here and ask if you would be willing to return to the manor to support Grace. Now I'm questioning if that's a good idea." Completely frustrated by his aunt's attitude regarding his marriage, he could feel his brow furrowing. She knew nothing about Grace and was making unfair assumptions.

"Actually, I think that's a wonderful idea," Aunt Hester said. "The marriage happened, and nothing can be done about it, so it will be best if I can have some time with your new wife to show her the way of things and give her some guidance on what it means to be a Carrington. Fear not, I'll bring her up to snuff. None of this was done properly, and you should know how much the appearance of propriety matters when you are a duke!"

Henry realized his aunt was vocalizing one of Grace's fears before they were married regarding the ways in which she did not feel she was qualified to be his duchess. Maybe she had a point and he should have listened to her more closely, but he did not for one second regret choosing to marry her.

"I can understand your concerns from the outside," he said, trying to placate his aunt. "Not knowing Grace, from the outside she may not seem like who you would consider a good match. But I assure you, I knew what I was doing when I decided to ask for her hand, and once you get to know her, you will see that she is a kind, empathetic, and intelligent woman who will make an outstanding duchess."

"I guess we shall see," his aunt responded with a sniff. "I'll prepare for travel today, and set off for Highland Manor tomorrow. I look forward to getting to know this woman you seem so passionate about. And don't you worry, I'll make her a worthy duchess for you."

After joining his aunt for tea, Henry left with some trepidation. Based on her initial negative thoughts toward Grace, he was not entirely sure asking her to return to the manor was the best idea. On the other hand, she was a wealth of knowledge about the family, the Carrington line, and maintaining tradition. Still settling into the role of duke himself, he knew the wisdom Aunt Hester could impart to Grace could help her feel more comfortable before they joined society next season.

CHAPTER 31

It had been a trying week since Henry's aunt had joined Grace at Highland Manor. She had first met the dowager the morning after she returned, and Grace had been polite, but reserved. Aunt Hester on the other hand was quick to speak her mind about the changes Grace had made and to comment on the areas where Grace needed to grow in order to present well as a duchess. Grace did not take offense, understanding her initial skepticism, and tried to present her kindest and most patient self to the dowager.

That first morning after Hester's arrival brought the first challenge for Grace. "Good morning, Aunt Hester," she said with a smile. "I hope you slept well. It must be nice to be back in your own bed after traveling."

"Good morning, Grace. I must admit it is nice to be home although I was enjoying time with friends, such a nice change of pace," the dowager said. Just then, two footmen entered the breakfast room, one placing a pot of tea in front of Aunt Hester, and the other placing steaming plates of food in front of them. "What's this? Where is the buffet?" Hester asked, eyes widening as she took in the plate.

"I've asked Mrs. Nelsen to prepare individual plates in the morning rather than the buffet to cut down on food waste and lighten the workload of the kitchen staff," Grace answered.

"Well, I never!" Hester replied, affronted. "Are we not able to choose what we wish to eat any longer?"

Examining her own plate, Grace could not see what all the fuss was about. It looked like a delectable plate of food with a slice of a mushroom, spinach, and onion quiche; some poached salmon in a dill cream sauce; a fresh summer tomato salad; and a rack of toast with fresh raspberry preserves on the side. "I think this looks delicious, the cook has outdone herself."

"That is not the point," Aunt Hester sputtered. "One wishes to have a say in what they consume in the morning. Besides, having a buffet is tradition, we have always had one as other ducal households do," she emphasized to Grace. "We must keep up appearances."

Taking a deep breath, Grace chose to leave the topic alone. It was not worth a fight. She returned her attention to the plate and enjoyed her food instead.

The peace only lasted a minute before Aunt Hester said to Grace, "I suppose now that you have married my nephew, you should tell me more about yourself."

She spent the next few minutes revealing how she had met Henry at Fitz and Moira's, suspecting Hester would approve of their having friends with a title.

Grace also shared an abbreviated version of her history, explaining her father's death, the aborted coming-out, her marriage to Lord Camden and subsequent time away from polite society in the north.

"I am sympathetic to what you have experienced," Aunt Hester said after Grace was done with her story. She looked a bit more contrite than previously. "It speaks well of you that the Countess of Geffen is a friend." Grace prevented herself from rolling her eyes at the expected response.

Staff returned to clear their plates away and Grace shared with Aunt Hester her plans to visit some of the tenant families that day as she was still getting to know them.

"You should be careful not to get too intimately involved with the tenants. Becoming too familiar can cause problems," Hester cautioned.

"What on earth are you talking about?" Grace was truly astonished by her response. "Henry said you have a strong tradition of care for the tenants."

"Care, yes," the dowager replied. "It is up to us as landlords to make sure those living on our land are happy and well taken care of. But there is a line we should not cross. It does no good to get too involved or they will come to rely on us too much. There is a certain distance that should be maintained between the classes."

"I'm afraid I don't share that sentiment," Grace said, becoming agitated with the woman's attitude. "I'm rather surprised you feel that way."

"Yes, well, judge me all you like," Hester sniffed.

"Things look different when you are in charge, and it would behoove you to remember that."

Yes, living with Aunt Hester was indeed a lesson in patience. She was never outright unkind to her, and Grace even suspected that over the past week she had begrudgingly come to like her. But oh, how she made comments. Many, many comments and moves behind the scenes.

The morning after Grace's initial breakfast with Aunt Hester, she noticed that the buffet was back. Letting it slide without comment in the moment, after the meal she went downstairs to inquire about the change.

"I'm so sorry, Your Grace," Mrs. Nelsen apologized. "The Dowager Duchess asked me about the changes to breakfast yesterday, and later in the day Standish asked me to change things back to how they had been before. I didn't know what to do as I can't go against Standish, I need to keep my position." The poor woman looked wretched, upset at being put in an unfair position. "I truly am sorry. If you want me to go back to individual plates, I can. Standish will understand if it's a directive from you."

"Please don't upset yourself Mrs. Nelsen," Grace sought to calm her. "For now, please continue to do as Standish asked. I don't want to create a rocky relationship with the dowager right from the start. In the grand scheme of things, it's really not a large enough issue to cause a commotion over." Mrs. Nelsen thanked her for being so understanding, and neither Grace nor Aunt Hester had commented on the presence of the breakfast buffet each subsequent morning. It did pique Grace learning that Standish was not in her corner, but rather was still devoted to the dowager.

Other comments continued throughout the week. Grace could only thank the good lord that the first parcel of dresses form the London Modiste had arrived the day before Aunt Hester had so she did not have to trot out any of her older dresses in front of the woman. Even so, there were more sniffs and comments about the plainness of the cut which Grace preferred, because as a duchess, she now must set the trend and be an example.

Beyond spending too much time getting to know the tenants, Aunt Hester also had an opinion on how Grace chose to spend her time. When she was found reading a volume of the history of agriculture to better understand what was happening on the estate, there was a comment about how she should leave the men's work to the men. When she found Grace in the kitchen gardens one day with a member of the kitchen staff, not being able to find fault with the activity outright, there was still a comment about it being unbecoming to cover herself in mud. This was conveyed, of course, with an accompanying sniff.

The dowager was not malicious in her delivery or intent, rather she was more concerned with maintaining appearances than either Henry or Grace, and she valued tradition more than anything. Grace could tell that there were times when she tried to restrain herself from commenting even further than she already did, yet she could not always help herself from

243

offering the advice which flowed out of her, putting Grace on edge.

Once Henry returned to Highland Manor, Grace tired talking to him about his aunt's interference when at the dowager's bequest, Standish once again countered changes she had initiated. It really shouldn't have mattered, each instance was just one small slight, but they were piling up and grating on her. Tossing and turning in bed that night, Henry had asked her what was wrong.

"I really am trying to love your aunt, but she makes it difficult," Grace said with a sigh.

"I know," Henry said. "We all just need to be patient with one another. She's helping us learn what it means to be a duke and duchess, and then she will be off to the Dower House before you know it. What's made you so upset in particular tonight?"

"A few weeks ago, when we first arrived, Mrs. Green mentioned that the last several deliveries of our linens were late being returned from the laundress. After inquiring, we discovered she was overrun with business and having trouble keeping up. So, with the blessing of our laundress, we decided to send out to another young woman in need of work."

"That sounds like a reasonable change to make, what was the problem?" Henry asked.

"It seems yesterday your aunt was not satisfied with the amount of starch in her handkerchief and set out to see why it was not up to her standards. When Mrs. Green told her of the change, she had the day's wash diverted back to the previous laundress." Grace let out a frustrated huff while Henry chuckled.

"I know you are irritated," he said, "but making a big deal of it only gives her more power. In the end, the laundry will be done, and isn't that what really matters?"

Retaining her composure, though he had entirely missed her point, Grace replied, "I know it's a small thing, but small things add up over time, and I don't like being questioned on everything I do in my own house."

"You are doing a wonderful job as duchess," Henry reassured her. "All of the staff and tenants love you, and Aunt Hester's opinions have not stopped you from doing anything, have they?" Henry made a valid point, but for the first time, it felt as if he was implying that Grace was being unreasonable, when previously he had always supported her.

Grace took a deep breath. Ever since realizing she had fallen in love with Henry, she could not help but look for signs he may feel the same way about her. He still showed her affection in a million little ways, but it hurt that he wouldn't stand up for her against his aunt, either ignoring her comments or rolling his eyes when the dowager could not see. She knew he was only trying to keep the peace, just as he had suggested she do, but by not taking a stand, she questioned if his feelings were as deep as what she felt for him.

CHAPTER 32

In mid-August, only a few days after Henry returned home, the political tensions that had been brewing finally erupted in Manchester. Henry was heartbroken as he read about the peaceful demonstrations on St. Peter's field turning violent—the magistrates, threatened by the crowd size, assaulting people for peacefully gathering to ask for representation in Parliament, discontent at the high prices of food that were driving some to starvation. Feeling their very way of life in danger, the Tories had allowed violence to rule the day, and now eleven people were dead and the ruling class in an even more perilous position.

Henry was not surprised at Reid's unannounced arrival the following day. Seeing him come up the drive, he went out to greet him. Reid frowned and rubbed his left thigh after swinging off the horse, then he walked toward Henry with a slight limp before clasping him in an embrace and slapping him on the back.

"It's good to see you, friend," Henry said as the two pulled away from each other. Henry noticed Reid grimace slightly as he shifted his weight back onto his legs. "The old war wound?" he asked.

"Yes," Reid bit out. "Unfortunately, the memory of Waterloo is never far behind."

"Come on in," he said, smartly choosing not to comment further. "Let's get you freshened up before you start the lectures on what happened in Manchester. And besides, Grace will be glad to see you." Henry led him through the house and back to the main drawing room where Grace and his aunt resided. He smiled at seeing Grace with her head buried in a book when they entered the room. His aunt, meanwhile, was participating in needlework, what he was sure she felt was the more appropriate pastime.

"We have a visitor," he announced as the men entered the room.

"Reid," Grace exclaimed, leaping to her feet, and embracing him. "It is so good to see you," she said as she beamed, choosing to ignore the sniff his aunt administered, no doubt at both the informality and familiarity of her greeting.

"I'm sorry to come unannounced," Reid apologized, "but I have urgent political business to discuss with Henry."

"Nonsense," Grace replied. "You know you are welcome here anytime. You're one of Henry's people, and that means you may as well be family. You never need to worry about announcing yourself."

The things this woman did to Henry's heart. It was the small things like Grace's easy acceptance of Reid that endeared her to him, and he struggled to see how his aunt still did not completely approve of her. While the dowager had grudgingly come around and recognized many of Grace's merits over the past few weeks, how could she still not understand that Grace was perfect for him?

"You must be exhausted from the road, did you come here straight from London?" Grace asked Reid.

"Yes, I set out just as dawn broke and practically wore out my horse."

"We'll get you both taken care of," Grace reassured him. Turning to address Standish who was waiting in the doorway, she said, "Standish, can you please have a bath drawn for the captain and make sure his bag is delivered to the green room? Will you also have the cook send up some snacks and ale?"

"Bless you, Grace," Reid said.

"But would you not prefer the gold room, Your Grace? That is usually where guests have been placed in the past," Standish interjected.

Henry saw Grace's face redden, but she remained polite yet firm when she responded. "No, I think the green room, as it has just been aired and will be more comfortable for the captain. Thank you, Standish." Dismissing the butler with authority, she left no doubt as to who was in charge. His aunt once again gave a sniff, and he wondered when Standish had begun questioning Grace.

Maybe Henry did need to pay more attention to how things had shifted for Grace since his aunt had retuned. He was wary of upsetting the tentative balance that had been established as he still valued Aunt Hester's insights and guidance when it came to how he should conduct himself now that he held the title. Henry wanted to honor his family's legacy, and that meant acting in a manner appropriate to his elevated position. However, hindering the closeness he had developed with Grace simply for the sake of what the *ton* thought was not an option.

He watched as Standish gave a stiff bow in acknowledgment and then gestured for Reid to follow him. Before making his way, Reid looked around the tense room, then shook his head while letting out a small grunt. Grace exited shortly after, posture stiff, announcing she was going to inform the cook that there would be an extra for dinner, and Henry wondered how his home had become such a minefield to navigate in his absence.

Two hours later the quartet was settled in the dining room. Reid filled Henry in on what was already being referred to as the Peterloo Massacre, and the reaction in London.

"Everyone is tense and scared that demonstrations and possibly even violence could also outbreak in the city," Reid said as he shoveled chicken into his mouth. "The Tories are clearly on the wrong side here, and their preemptive action has showed their hand. The laboring class can see those in charge are scared the events in France could be replicated here, and the ruling class obliterated. It's hard for working men and women to see the purpose of the peerage when they are struggling to put food on their tables."

Reid was gesturing wildly in his passion on the subject, unmindful that he was still holding his knife. Grace, sitting next to him, gently removed it from his grip and set it on the edge of his plate. Reid gave her a sheepish smile before continuing. "The irony here, is that by stepping in when the crowd was still peaceful, and creating chaos which led to death, the masses are now closer than ever to the breaking point. The attempt to quell may be the catalyst for what pushes them closer to trying to dismantle those at the top—the urge to suppress has only heightened the danger."

"Are there any immediate measures that can be taken to help those who are suffering most?" Grace asked. "Since governmental reform takes time, can we not open reserves of food stores set aside for the army to help fill the need? Perhaps lessening tensions until more permanent solutions can be passed through Parliament is a way forward."

Listening, Henry was once again struck by Grace's compassion. He greatly admired her care for those outside her own class when so many believed they should remain separate. Many in the peerage didn't spare a thought for those who supported them and made their lives easier every day. Just as he was appreciating his wife, his aunt spoke up, dismissing Grace and trying to correct her.

"Women should not involve themselves in politics, my dear," Aunt Hester said. "It is a man's place and unseemly for us to get involved."

Henry watched as Grace stiffened, anticipating an impassioned counterargument from her, women's education and independence being near to her heart. But she said nothing, not acquiescing to what his aunt had said, but not challenging her either, looking down at her plate with pursed lips. He felt uneasy seeing her moderate herself and was about to speak up on her behalf when Reid beat him to it.

"I have to most respectfully disagree with you, Your Grace," he said to the dowager. "I think it behooves women to understand what is happening in the world around them, and we men might be better served if we also had the input of feminine wisdom from time to time." At this, he smiled at Grace. "Meaningful change will never arise unless we listen to other perspectives. If men were to think with that kind of compassion more often, we may be able to solve problems in a timelier manner. Instead, we are usually too stubborn to even try and understand the perspective of those we believe to be on the other side of an issue. Conflicts are not resolved easily if we refuse to look at other options."

"Here, here," Henry affirmed, glad to see Grace smiling at him. Wanting to see that smile more often, he resolved to make Grace more at ease and comfortable with herself as she had before he was forced to leave. She was what mattered most to him now, and he would do anything to make her happy.

———

Grace enjoyed having Reid in the house. He brought a levity with him that eased the growing tension in the household and proved to be a wonderful distraction. More than anything, though, she wanted to escape with Henry and return to how it had been when they were first married, when the intimacy between them had been easy and they were able to focus on one another and live as they wished. Now, with their isolation broken and every action questioned, the ease was gone. She was not sure if the foundation they had laid together would be secure enough to keep them standing for much longer. Grace worried that the pressure to be like everyone else and maintain the status quo of the aristocracy when they returned to London in the new year would only exacerbate matters. Surrounded by the *ton* and subsumed into polite society, would they lose themselves completely and become lost among the crowd?

Though Henry had not spoken of his aunt's initial reaction to their marriage, Grace could guess it was not warm based on the comments Hester made when they first met. It was clear the dowager agreed with many of the reasons she feared she was not an equal match to Henry and had at first resisted him. When proposing, Henry asserted that his position in society would overcome her lack of connections, and she had allowed herself to believe him because the picture of the future he had painted was what she had always desired.

If Grace was honest with herself, looking back, she could recognize that even then she had been falling for Henry. As resistant as she had been to the idea of marrying again, a small part of herself wanted the fairytale: a good man who saw and loved her for who she was. But they were both naïve in their understanding of how polite society operated, having been on the fringes for so long. She still worried the judgment of others could keep them from influencing the kind of changes they both desired.

Reid believed that Henry could have a profound influence within the House of Lords as a duke, which was why he was here to discuss strategy after the tragedy in Manchester. Change was inevitable if they did not wish for an uprising similar to what had occurred in the American colonies and France. Reid was trying to champion for expanding representation, which was vital if England wanted to avoid further war within its own borders. Utilizing Henry's new position was a key part of that strategy. But Grace knew Henry's efforts would be in vain if he did not have the respect of his peers due to his choice of wife.

If Aunt Hester's attitude as a member of the *ton* was any indication, Grace had become an albatross around Henry's neck. She refused to make him powerless, and as much as she loved him, if it was clear that she would harm more than help, she would need to leave him for the greater good.

Two days later, Reid's stay abruptly ended in the

middle of luncheon after he received a note from a frantic delivery boy.

"What is it?" Henry asked, concern creasing his brow. "More trouble similar to Manchester?"

"No," Reid said tonelessly, laying the letter on the table and staring unseeing into the distance. His calm façade twisted into a grimace while he uttered a quiet curse. Taking a deep breath, he said, "It appears my father died last week, and I am being summoned back to the family estate. I never wanted this, but I'm now the Earl of Weston . . ." Grace did not know the history involved, but it was clear from Reid's troubled expression that the relationship to his new position was complicated, and like Henry, he had reservations about assuming his title.

"This is the last thing I need right now," a frustrated Reid said. "With everything that's going on, I should be focused on what we will present to Parliament next year. Now I won't even be able to press for change from my seat in Commons, as I'll have to resign as MP and serve in Lords. Damn it!" He slammed his hand down on the table, causing the glasses to shake. "I'm sorry, please forgive me, Your Grace," he said to Grace with a contrite smile.

Tugging at his hair, he dropped his head into his hands for a moment before looking up at Henry. "My influence has just been greatly diminished, as my vote will now be drowned out in Lords with the Whigs holding such a minority. We'll need to rely on Sidney to whip the House of Commons into line, and I'm going to need you to persuade those most entrenched in their ways in Lords."

Reid's words sinking in, Grace took a shaky breath, realizing the stakes had just become even higher. She was more of a liability to Henry now than ever before.

CHAPTER 33

Reid left early the next morning to ride back to London and meet with his father's lawyers before returning to his childhood home. Henry felt for him, he knew how difficult it was transitioning into a title, especially since Reid had not spoken with his father in several years and had no idea the current condition of the estate he was now in charge of. He also knew Reid took great pride in his role as an MP and would loath relinquishing it to claim his seat in the House of Lords, an increasingly archaic body. The two men shook hands as Reid's mount was brought around, and Henry gave him a quick salute before he rode down the drive.

Making his way into the house, Henry went to find Grace in the library. He had felt a distance growing between them ever since his aunt had arrived, but she seemed especially agitated about something in the past few days and he wanted to learn what was disturbing her. He desperately wanted to bring back the closeness he had felt with her when it had been just the two of them at the manor, allowing Grace to drop her many walls and trust him.

The first few weeks of their marriage he had been allowed to show her open affection and care for her the way he wanted. Now that his aunt had joined them, whenever he tried to lay his hand on her or kiss her temple as he passed her, his aunt would sniff in disapproval, as affection for one's wife was thought improper in the *ton*. While Aunt Hester's thoughts on the matter were not enough to dissuade him, Grace now stiffened away from him when he approached her. Even though they still shared a bed each night, she rarely allowed him to hold her, and they had not made love since he returned, increasing the distance between them.

His plans to turn things around were brought up short, though, when he found his aunt was also in the library. Picking up on an uneasy air in the room, he observed Grace sitting in the window seat. Though she was holding an open book in her lap, she stared at the pages with unseeing eyes, her body rigid. He started to make his way toward her, but having seen him enter the room, his aunt called out to him and halted his progress.

"Oh, Henry, good!" she proclaimed. "I was just telling Grace she should read more appropriate texts. Can you believe she even wanted to read this?" She was waving a volume at him as if the motion alone could invoke his outrage. Without a word, he reached over and pulled the book out of her hand to see what had so offended her. His heart dropped when he recognized the author's name, Mary Wollstonecraft.

Stroking the leather spin, he said, "I gave this book to Grace as a gift." He looked up, locking eyes with her. "I don't see anything wrong with her choosing to read it."

Aunt Hester opened her mouth, but before a confrontation Henry believed was long overdue could commence, a rap on the door alerted them to Standish's presence. The normally unruffled butler looked slightly put out, if his pursed lips were any indication, and Grace rose to inquire what he needed.

"Another unexpected guest has arrived and asked to see you, Your Grace. What would you have me do with him?"

Aunt Hester sniffed loudly and interjected, "Just as one is leaving, another has arrived? Really, Grace, you must run a tighter ship."

Henry seethed at the way his aunt and Standish were expressing their disapproval of Grace. It was preposterous, as she could not control who arrived at their door and when. He saw Grace color at the criticism, but she simply paused for a moment before straightening her posture and responding to Standish, choosing to ignore his aunt's slight.

"You said they wished to see me—who is it that has arrived?" Grace asked, voice polite.

"He announced himself as the Earl of Camden and said he was a relation of yours, Your Grace," Standish said with a barely concealed sneer. Upon hearing who had called, Grace paled, but quietly asked Standish to see him to the drawing room and to order some tea and refreshments. When Standish left, Grace sank into the nearest chair. Henry rushed to her side. Crouching down in front of her, he clasped her hands between his.

"What is he doing here?" she asked in disbelief. "There is no reason we should need to further our acquaintance."

"Let's go and see why he has turned up unannounced. I'm coming with you, I'll not allow you to face him alone," Henry stated firmly, rubbing his thumb along the back of her hand.

She smiled warmly, looking like her old self, and he basked in it. "Thank you," she said, bringing a hand up to cup his cheek. And for a moment, it was the two of them against the world again. "Let's go then," she said, putting on a brave face and breaking the spell. He reached out a hand, pulling her from the chair, and she held on as they made their way to the drawing room.

Grace tugged on his hand to stop him as they passed the stairs leading down to the kitchen. "I need to inform Mrs. Nelsen and Mrs. Green we will have a guest for the evening." She must have seen the displeased look on his face, because she answered him before he could even ask the question of whether the man should stay. "I don't want him here either," she said, "but it's too late in the day to send him back out on the road with another summer storm brewing. You know I'm right." He grudgingly agreed and waited for her at the edge of the kitchen.

"I'm sorry to make you cook for one more on such short notice again," Grace said to Mrs. Nelsen.

"It's not a problem at all," the cook reassured her. "I was planning to make up the fresh trout that was delivered this morning, and there is more than enough to go around."

"That sounds wonderful. Can you please prepare it with the lemon sauce?" With Mrs. Nelsen's agreement, they headed back upstairs to face the unwelcome guest.

When they reached the door of the drawing room, Grace paused to smooth out her hair and dress. Taking a deep breath, she straightened her posture and nodded for Henry to open the door. Upon entering the room, they saw a man sitting on the settee who rather resembled a rodent, with his pinched face.

"Ah, Your Grace, it's a pleasure to meet you," he said, standing to give a quick bow in Henry's direction. "And cousin Grace."

"I'm not your cousin," she blurted in a clipped tone. "What are you doing here, my lord?"

With a smarmy smile, he said, "I just learned of your marriage, and I simply had to come and offer my congratulations."

Still standing, not granting their guest the courtesy of sitting down for a more formal conversation, Grace said, "I wrote to you of my engagement and impending marriage four weeks ago, this cannot be new information to you."

Shuffling slightly, but still falsely smiling, he said, "Yes, but I just heard that it was His Grace you married." He gave a forced laugh before gritting out, "You neglected to mention that part in your letter."

Looking him straight in the eye, Grace bluntly said,

"So you did not come here to offer your congratulations, but rather to ingratiate yourself to my husband, the duke."

Henry's cheeks hurt from how wide he was smiling, and he wouldn't have been able to hold back the grin if he had tired. He had never been prouder as his wife confront this small-minded man who had tried to make her believe she didn't matter. Even in the midst of feeling insecure in her own home, she had found her confidence again and was standing up for herself. It was a beautiful thing to behold.

As Camden spluttered, Henry spoke up for the first time. "I am well aware of the dismissive way you treated my wife when she found herself in need of support after your cousin's death, my lord." Staring the other man down, he added, "As well as how you propositioned her and sought to use her vulnerability." The man swallowed at Henry's unforgiving tone. "I'm enough of a gentleman that I will not proactively disparage or slight you in society, but you can be assured that I will *never* speak up for you or lend my favor."

He took Grace's hand and looked at her fondly. "My wife, being the kind soul that she is, has arranged a room for you to stay with us for the night, as the weather is about to turn foul. We will allow you to join us for dinner tonight, but you will be on your way as soon as the weather clears, and this will be the last night you ever spend in this house."

Before Camden could respond, a knock sounded on the door and a maid entered with a tea tray. "Marie,"

Grace said, "Lord Camden will be retiring to his room until dinner. Would you mind taking the tea tray up to the room Mrs. Green has assigned him? He will follow you there." Camden sent a look of utter loathing toward Grace and followed the maid out of the room, knowing he had been dismissed.

The entire confrontation had lasted only minutes, yet as soon as the drawing room door closed, Grace slumped against Henry, completely drained of all energy. He wrapped his arms around her and relished in her touch. "You were bloody marvelous," he said into her hair. Feeling her start to shake, he worried she was crying until he heard her snort and realized she was laughing.

"Oh," she gasped, "that felt wonderful. To be able to actually put that horrible man in his place."

"I mean it," he said, cradling her face. "You are incredible." Henry delighted at the light he saw shining in her eyes and he leaned forward to claim her mouth in a kiss.

CHAPTER 34

The summer storm was rumbling away outside as Grace sat down to dinner with her husband and their uninvited guest. She hoped they would make it through the meal without anyone wanting to kill one another. After everything that had happened over the past dozen or so days when the dowager had arrived, Grace was emotionally exhausted and could not endure making small talk. Even though Aunt Hester was staring daggers at Grace for not living up to her expectations of a polite hostess, she couldn't bring herself to care and let the dowager converse with Camden throughout the salad and soup courses.

Grace tried to make herself focus and follow the discussion, but her mind kept wandering to the ways she was failing to be what Henry needed. He had been so sweet and supportive of her when Camden had first arrived, and before when defending her choice of reading material. For a few moments she had thought that maybe they could make this work between them.

But in the end, trying to save their marriage would only make things worse when she inevitably besmirched Henry's family name, ruining his chance to create the kind of change he desired.

As one of the footmen placed the main course in front of her, she pulled herself back to attention. Picking up her fork to take a bite of the wonderful-looking trout, she realized that the dish was not prepared as she had asked.

"Stop!" she cried, startling everyone at the table. Henry turned and looked at her with wide eyes, and Aunt Hester's fork clattered to her plate as she dropped it in surprise. "Don't eat the fish!" she implored.

"Child, what is the matter with you!" Aunt Hester exclaimed.

Ignoring the dowager, she turned her full attention to their guest. "Lord Camden, did you eat any of the fish?" she asked with a note of desperation in her voice.

"I only managed one bite before you so rudely yelled at all of us," he said in a huff.

"Grace, what's wrong?" Henry said, looking at her with concern.

Noticing that Camden's face was starting to bloom mottled splotches, she frantically turned to the footman who was serving that evening. "Simon, what did Mrs. Nelson tell you was the main course this evening?"

Bewildered, the footman answered, "Trout almondine, Your Grace."

"Almonds!" Camden spat through slightly labored breathing. "Are you trying to poison me, you witch?"

Everyone began to speak at once. Henry raged at Camden for daring to speak to her in such a manner, Camden was yelling about what a vile person she was as he clawed at his collar, and Aunt Hester demanded to know what was going on.

"Enough!" Grace yelled, surprising even herself and bringing all others to a stop. "Lord Camden is allergic to nuts. Simon, I need you to go and fetch the nearest doctor as fast as you can. Henry, let's help him up to his room."

Chaos reigned, but in a matter of seconds everyone snapped into action. Hearing the commotion, Standish entered the dining room and assisted Henry with getting Lord Camden upstairs. Grace followed them up once she had obtained the medical supplies Mrs. Green kept on hand. Slightly wheezing and covered in a rash, Lord Camden certainly did not look well. But having ingested so little of the food, and considering he'd been yelling for the past hour while waiting for the doctor, Grace did not believe his life was in danger.

The doctor confirmed as much when he arrived and made Camden more comfortable with a cream for his rash and a breathing treatment. After a few hours, Camden fell asleep and the doctor left, telling them to keep an eye on him overnight and repeat the breathing treatment if necessary. Grace went into the hallway, and finally having a moment to relax, covered her face with her hands before sinking to the floor, lacking the energy to move. Henry and Standish appeared a moment later, and the second the door was fully closed, Henry turned to confront the butler.

"How on earth did this happen?" Henry whispered angrily. Standish recoiled at the look of rage on Henry's face, and even Grace was a bit intimidated, not used to seeing him so riled. "I specifically heard Her Grace instruct Mrs. Nelsen this morning that she was to serve the trout with lemon sauce. Why was the menu changed without consulting her? That is the standard procedure, is it not?"

Standish, quickly replacing his mask of placidity that all good butlers possess, answered him calmly. "Your Grace, Mrs. Nelsen informed me this afternoon that she did not have enough lemons and needed to make a change to the main course. She proposed trout almondine and asked me to get approval for the change, as Mrs. Green was away at the time."

"You never came to me for approval, Standish." Grace spoke up from her position on the floor, startling the men who had been too preoccupied to notice her. "I never would have approved the dish, as I knew of Lord Camden's sensitivity," she said, appalled by the communication breakdown.

"I obtained approval for the change from the dowager duchess, Your Grace," Standish replied in a matter-of-fact tone.

"Why on earth did you go to my aunt rather than Her Grace?" Henry asked, seething.

Standish, not comprehending the issue, calmly said, "The Dowager has more experience entertaining, Your Grace. I trusted she would know what an appropriate meal would be to represent a ducal household to our guest."

Grace felt her heart shatter at Standish's answer. It was her worst fears come to fruition in what could have been a life-threatening situation. Neither Standish nor the dowager trusted Grace to do what was best for Henry, or to not disgrace the title. If the people closest to Henry could not support her, then no one else would either.

"That is all for tonight, Standish. We will continue this conversation tomorrow. You are dismissed," Henry said. With a bow, Standish walked away.

"Are you alright?" Henry asked as he knelt beside her. His anger seemed to have dissipated with Standish's retreat, and he now had nothing but concern in his eyes as he looked at her. Unable to speak, she simply nodded. "I know that was quite the evening. Come, let's go to our room. We'll be alerted if anything else is needed for Camden." He stood and helped her to her feet.

Grace couldn't bring herself to say anything as they entered Henry's bedchamber. She had a lump in her throat and was trying to prevent herself from breaking down into tears. She knew what she needed to do. There was no question anymore; the events of this evening made it crystal clear that she would not be able to overcome her shortcomings and support Henry in the way he needed. No one would ever respect her as a duchess, and she would hinder his ability to make the changes so many were counting on for their livelihoods. As much as it would break her heart, now that she had finally found love after missing it for so long, she had to leave him.

Grace watched as Henry began to unbutton his waistcoat, beginning preparations for bed and not bothering to call Smyth at such a late hour. She stood there, unable to do anything other than look at him and drink him in, trying to memorize the details of his face and his form. He was so beautiful that it made her heart ache, and before she could stop it, a tear rolled down her cheek.

A moment later, noticing she had not moved, Henry looked up at her. Seeing she was frozen just inside the door, he made his way back toward her and rubbed his hands up and down her arms in a comforting gesture. "Hey," he said, dipping his head so he could look her in the eyes, "are you sure you're alright, you haven't said a thing."

"No," she told him. "I'm not alright." She couldn't stop the tears now and they began to flow down her face as the wall she had tried to erect, acting like a dam, failed behind the weight of her feelings. "Henry, this isn't working. You have to let me go."

CHAPTER 35

Not understanding what Grace was trying to say, but stunned by the implication of her words, Henry tried to keep himself calm. "What do you mean? What are you talking about?"

He was scared to ask the question but thought it might be worse if he did not know for certain. He could not fight for what mattered to him, which was unequivocally her, if he did not fully understand what he was fighting for.

"We thought we would be able to make a marriage between us a success, but the events of this evening have only brought clarity to what I have been feeling for a few days now. We gambled too freely, and the cost is too high," she said, trying to sound resolute. Horrified, he could see that she genuinely believed what she was saying.

"Tell it to me plainly," he insisted, needing to be certain. "Are you saying you don't want to be in this marriage anymore?" His voice cracked with pent up emotion after a trying evening, and he watched her wince as if physically pained by his question.

"What I'm saying is that I'm a liability to you," she whispered, her eyes still closed.

"You are not a liability," he said incredulously. Grace opened her eyes, silently pleading with him. "How can you think that?" he asked. "You make me better. I'm so much happier since I met you—I feel more at home here and more comfortable as the duke."

"Yes," she agreed. "It's good when it's just us. But we don't live in isolation Henry. Before we were married, I was worried how others would react to me as your choice of wife. There was a lot working against me that did not make me an obvious choice." She lowered her gaze, and he could physically see her old uncertainties making themselves at home.

"Ever since your aunt joined us," she continued, "I've seen that my fears were not unfounded. If even those who are closest to you and should be your greatest supporters cannot accept me, then others outside your circle will never do so." She calmed with each word, tears lessening and her conviction growing stronger. But every now and then a tear still escaped, illustrating her inner struggle.

His heart breaking, Henry chose his words carefully, wanting to reassure her and make the case that she was not seeing circumstances clearly. "I won't pretend that my aunt didn't voice some concerns about you when I first approached her. But once she met you, she could see what a good person you are, and she started to warm to you. I know she has been judgmental and questioned some of the changes we both wish to make, but that doesn't mean she doesn't like you."

"It's not about whether or not she likes me as a person," Grace insisted. "I'm aware that she no longer thinks I tried to entrap you in marriage, and she may even grudgingly feel I am a good person, but that's not the problem Henry. If that was all that was at stake, I could live with her slights."

"Then what is the problem? I don't see how this can't be fixed by me having an overdue conversation with Aunt Hester." He was growing frustrated, not seeing why she thought their marriage had failed because his aunt liked to issue cutting comments too frequently.

"The problem," Grace said, weariness creeping into her voice, "is that she doesn't respect me." She paused and looked at him to make sure her words had sunk in. "The comments and questions aren't about her not liking me as person," she explained, "they are meant to undermine me because she does not see me as someone capable of being a duchess. Even Standish doesn't regard me as the head of this household. You heard him tonight. He didn't even bother to seek me out for a housekeeping matter, instead he went straight to your aunt because he views her as the one who should be making decisions."

He sucked in a breath as her words hit him like a punch to the gut. He recalled what she had told him about how his aunt had reversed changes Grace had made, but since they would not have a significant impact, had not seen them as issues that really mattered. But the fact that his aunt had been able to have her way and overrode Grace's wishes did, and he had missed it, not understanding where her growing distress had come from.

Henry had been outraged at the situation Standish had caused this evening, even if he did not mind Camden suffering a bit. Grace was absolutely right that the butler never should have gone to his aunt. He started to see instances he had observed himself in a different light. How Standish had addressed her with less than complete respect when Camden had arrived today, and openly questioned her instructions regarding Reid. And Standish had turned to him as the voice of authority when Grace fought for the boys on staff to keep their place.

What a fool he had been. Before she agreed to marry him, he promised her that she would oversee the household and run it the way she desired because he understood her need to create the life she wanted after having been relegated to the sidelines for so many years. And what had happened? He had allowed both his aunt and the head of his staff to undermine her. He had allowed circumstances that once again made her feel like she did not matter in her own home and had unwittingly undercut the confidence she was fighting so hard to reclaim.

"I'm so sorry, Grace," he said. He squeezed his eyes shut and leaned down to rest his forehead on hers, intertwining their fingers, wanting to feel the slightest connection to her. "I should have seen it was deeper than just some snide comments. I saw how it was affecting you and I had planned to talk to my aunt, but I should have spoken up for you sooner." He sucked in a ragged breath, pausing to compose himself and find the right words. "You asked me to let you run your life as you wished when we married, and I've let you down. But I can fix this, Grace. In no uncertain terms, I'll make clear to Standish, my aunt, and the entire staff that you are now the duchess. They will respect and answer only to you. We don't need to separate over this."

"Henry, I believe that you can fix things here because everyone in this household ultimately answers to you and will do as you instruct them to," she said, disentangling one of her hands from his and laying it across his cheek. "But what has happened here at Highland Manor is only a symptom of a larger problem," she continued, looking him dead in the eyes. "Like it or not, you are now a duke, and you have a larger role to fulfill. You wield influence on those around you, which is what made you believe my insufficiencies would be overlooked. But that influence only works if they respect you and hold you in esteem."

She closed her eyes, a pained expression on her face as she continued. "Living through the past few weeks and seeing how your aunt and Standish have reacted to me has exposed how others within polite society will as well, and you will not be able to command all of them to show me respect as you can here. There is too much working against me. I will only bring you down and lessen what you can achieve."

Starting to panic, Henry could tell how deadly serious she was. "They just need to get to know you," he said urgently. "You've never been out in society. People don't know who you are. Once they get to know you, they will love you. You said yourself that even my aunt is coming around."

"That may be true in time, but as we already established, liking someone is not the same as respecting them. And you don't have the luxury of time. I know how much you wish to make changes in this country, to see progress made in the way we farm and do business so that innovations can be made. You know there are inequalities that must be addressed soon to appease the laboring class, just look at Peterloo. Your influence within the peerage is needed now, but it won't matter if no one takes you seriously. The wives of the very lords you need on your side will titter about me behind their fans in London ballrooms, and it will diminish you in their eyes for choosing a wife so poorly."

Henry didn't know what to say. He could tell she was absolutely convinced of the argument she was making. "What if none of that matters to me?" he said desperately.

She laughed and began crying again. "You don't mean that, nor can you expect me to believe it. I know you Henry—you have always wanted to help others and to serve England. It's why you joined the army when the country was under the threat of war. It's why you continued to work for the government in the war department even after you were no longer actively deployed on the continent. Long before you had the chance to influence change in Parliament, you wanted the opportunity to make a difference. It's one of the reasons I love you so much. You care about people more than yourself. Now you have the chance to make significant change, so don't try and tell me it doesn't matter.

"You love me?" he asked, completely astonished. He knew he needed to clarify that it was *she* who mattered more than anything else he might do, but he was too preoccupied by what she had said to explain at that moment.

"Yes, I love you," she affirmed. "I love you for wanting to make everything around you better. I love you for seeing me when no one else would and for showing me what a marriage should be. But just because you can see me, it doesn't mean you can make the rest of the world see me as well. And it's because of that, and because I do love you, that I must leave. So that you can be the man you are meant to be, without me holding you back."

She let out a shuddering breath before offering her final word. "I know we cannot simply dissolve our marriage, but we can live separately, and soon my tarnish will wear off you. I'll go live at another of your properties. You can inform me which one you think best. I'll begin preparations to leave in the morning." She leaned in and placed a lingering kiss on his cheek. "I'm going to bed, this day has exhausted me."

And with that blow to his heart, she walked out of his room.

CHAPTER 36

"Aunt Hester!" Henry shouted, pounding on her bedroom door, not caring that it was past midnight. "Aunt Hester, I need to talk to you!" He was in a blind panic ever since Grace had left his room. He'd tried to get her to talk to him more, knocking on the door between their rooms and pleading with her that it didn't need to be over. When she didn't answer him, he went down the hall to find his aunt in a state of distress.

The door finally opened a crack, and he could faintly see his aunt in the dim candlelight as she stood in her dressing gown, clearly upset at being roused from sleep. "What are you hollering about at such an hour? Has something happened to Lord Camden?" she asked as she peered into the hallway behind him.

"I need to talk to you," he said urgently, pushing past her into the room. Pacing in front of the fire remnants, Henry pulled at his hair in agitation. "Grace says that she wants to leave because she doesn't think that you or Standish respect her," he said bluntly, far too upset to mince his words. Aunt Hester looked taken aback by his assertion, but sensing he needed to vent his feeling, she sat down in a chair without saying a word. "She has it in her mind that because of her background, the *ton* won't accept her and that I won't be able to influence change in the House of Lords or society. She thinks she is holding me back, and the cold welcome you graced her with has only reinforced her deepest fears."

"Oh, dear," she said softly, looking a bit contrite.

"Oh, dear?" he parroted back in an unbelieving tone. "Is that all you have to say? This is all your fault."

She snapped her head up and looked at him with a flinty gaze. "Sit down!" she barked. "I'll let that slide as you are clearly upset, but I think it's time for some hard truths to be aired." When he finally sat in the armchair across from her, she sighed. "Hard truths for both of us I think."

"What does that mean?" Henry inquired more calmly.

"It means that I knew you were not prepared to take over the dukedom, as no one had ever thought so many tragedies would occur for it to be within your reach. I couldn't help you at first because I was so lost in my own grief." She was quiet for a moment, looking down lost in thought before saying, "It's a terrible thing to lose a child. I had already lost so many, but Michael thrived. He grew to be a man and I saw a future in him.

I was not prepared for how it would be to lose him as well . . . I was supposed to go first." She paused for a moment to compose herself.

"I was ill-equipped to help you transition into your role, and I allowed myself space because I thought I had time to teach you. I was shocked when I received your letter informing me that you were planning to marry. I knew my time wallowing in my own sadness needed to end, so I pulled myself together and came back when you asked me to. I already felt at a disadvantage not knowing your wife, and I can admit that I overreacted."

"Thank you for saying that," Henry said gently. Hearing his aunt discuss how profoundly her life had changed reminded him he was not the only one affected by the dramatic changes in their family. "If you knew you had been unfair to her, then why have you been so relentlessly critical of her since you came home?"

"Because she needed to learn as well," his aunt answered. "I understood as soon as I met her what it was you saw in her, and I could see it too," she admitted. "Grace could be a wonderful wife and support for you, but she needs to understand her role. I see I might have taken things a bit far, but any time I questioned her, it was because I was trying to make her think about how her choices and actions would appear to others. The hard truth that neither of you seem to understand is that when trying to navigate the peerage, appearances and connections do matter."

"But they shouldn-," Henry started to speak but was silenced by his aunt's raised hand.

"I'm not saying they should matter, only that they do, and you ignore that fact at your peril. Your wife is not entirely wrong, she will be judged for her short-comings, and you will be judged for choosing a wife who does not fit the expected mold. You have been too quick to dismiss her valid concerns about the inequality in your union, and I was trying—though maybe not in the most useful way—to help you see that there would be objections you needed to prepare for."

"I can understand that to a point as far as comments on conduct or appearance are concerned," he said, "but why undermine her with the staff and set Standish against her?" Henry asked, truly puzzled. "One of the only things she asked of me before we were married was to allow her to run her own house as she saw fit, and I promised her that much. Now, though, she feels powerless in her own home because you and Standish have been making changes without her knowledge or approval."

Looking rather abashed, Hester answered, "That was unintentional, but my fault. I did not mean to undercut Grace, I just found it harder than I thought it would be to relinquish control of the running of the household. It had been my domain for twenty years you know, and it was hard to see her making changes to how things were run. Standish, having always been loyal to me, followed the lead I had unwittingly set. I realized how out of hand things had become tonight with the fiasco at dinner. I never should have approved the menu changes, as it was not my place, and Standish never should have come to me. I'll talk with him in the morning and offer Grace my apologies."

"No," Henry said firmly, "I will talk with Standish in the morning. But I still don't know what to do about Grace. Do you really think she's right about her negatively impacting my ability to effect change?" He was at a loss, in danger of veering into despair. "I can't lose her," he said. "I love her . . ."

"Does she know that?" she asked, staring him down intently. When he didn't answer, she added, "Maybe you should tell her."

Henry hung his head, knowing she was right. He'd had the chance earlier that evening to tell Grace how he felt but had failed to tell her, shattered by the idea she felt leaving him was for the best. He did love her, and she was the most important thing in his life—he would do whatever he needed for her to understand that and to stay. "Is there anything I can do to show her that she belongs with me, that we can face whatever happens together?" he asked his aunt, desperate for any hope she might provide.

"You asked me a minute ago if I really think she is right, and I do." She reached over and lifted his chin so he was looking at her. "But that does not mean that the problem is insurmountable. The two of you may not know how the *ton* works, but I do. Yes, appearances and reputation are important, but the best way to influence others is simply to speak and act with conviction. That is part of what I was trying to teach both of you these past weeks. You can make changes if you think they are important. Not all traditions are made equal." Henry was dumbfounded, and she gave him no opportunity to respond. "I know you've been concerned about the family legacy and not doing anything to harm the Carrington name, but maintaining tradition is not the only way, or even the best way, to do that. Part of the reason I challenged both you and Grace was to make you stand up for yourselves and back your convictions. You were both so worried about upsetting the apple cart that neither of you stood up for yourselves or one another."

With that truth ringing in his head, Henry felt like he could finally breathe, a weight off his chest. He had been holding back out of fear of what others would think if he ran things a different way, contradicting his desire to seek change. But if being a duke meant acting with authority and conviction, knowing you were secure in your place at the top of the peerage, then all of Grace's fears meant nothing as long as they held firm to what they believed and stood strong in their power. He would not abuse his title to get what he wanted, he would simply use his influence to stand by her and rise above any petty comments. By not allowing others' opinions to move him from what he knew was right, he would show his strength and maintain his position of influence.

With a sharp look, Aunt Hester studied him while he was lost in thought. "I can see that finally set in," she commented. "Now, what is it that matters the most, and what are you going to fight for?"

"I want to win Grace back," he said without hesitation. "Without her, none of it matters."

"Good," Aunt Hester said, "let's make a plan."

CHAPTER 37

Grace's eyes were gritty from all the tears she had shed, and her head felt heavy, filled with a thick fog that made it hard to think clearly. Perched in the window seat in her room, arms wrapped around her legs, she watched the dawn arriving. She had barely slept, remembering the look on Henry's face when she told him with finality that she would be leaving and remembering his voice as he spoke to her through the door, pleading for her to talk with him. But there was no point in another discussion. Talking again and belaboring the issue would only make everything harder on both of them.

She had not intended to tell him that she loved him, it had just slipped out in her desperation to make him understand. He hadn't said it back, but in many ways, his silence on the subject was easier. She could leave knowing his heart was not breaking as completely as hers.

A light knock sounded at the door. It could only be

Lucy that early in the morning, so she called for her to enter. Looking up, Grace was surprised to see it was the dowager. "Aunt Hester, I wasn't expecting you."

Walking into the room and assessing Grace, she said, "You look like you've had better days."

"It was a rather long evening," Grace replied. "I do hope that Lord Camden is feeling better this morning."

"I'm sure he's fine," Aunt Hester quipped, "but I don't think that's the only thing that happened last night." When Grace remained silent, she continued. "And are you still planning on leaving my nephew this morning?"

Grace looked down, blushing at the question. "I don't really think I have an option," she replied. "I thought you of all people would understand. I don't want to hold him back."

"Because you love him," Hester stated.

Grace looked up again in surprise, startled by the blunt statement. If that was how Hester wanted to play it, she may as well be honest herself. "Yes," she said simply.

Sighing, Aunt Hester sat down on the edge of the bed. "You two fools. You can't get out of your own way," she said while shaking her head. "But first I think I need to apologize to you." Grace was shocked, but she didn't show it, choosing to let the woman continue. "I judged you unfairly when I first met you, but most of that had nothing to do with you. It was a reflection of my own state of mind as I was trying to emerge from my grief. I jumped to conclusions based on what little information I had learned about you. But as soon as I met you, I knew you had not tried to take advantage of Henry as I had feared. Unlike most of the social climbers out there, you are not showy about your new standing and the accouterments now at your disposal. I could see that you were a good match for Henry, as you both see the world in much the same way, so I decided to try and whip you into shape on the duchess front. As you know, appearances matter."

"I thought you didn't approve of me," Grace said in wonder. She could hardly believe what she was hearing. She knew the dowager had warmed to her, but she had no inclination the dowager felt she was a good match for Henry.

"I suppose I'm rather blunt and may not have approached the lessons in the right way," Aunt Hester admitted. "As I told Henry, it was not my intention to undercut you and your place in the house. I understand why being mistress of your own home is important to you, and I'm sorry I made you question my respect for you and the position you now hold. I think it was more of an adjustment than I realized to let go of the reigns. But you need to know that I don't disapprove of you, I just want to prepare you for what is to come." She eyed Grace with a knowing look. "You're a shrewd one. You understood the challenges that you would face when being presented to society in ways my nephew could not. But dear girl, those challenges are not enough to end a marriage over."

"I don't see a way around it," Grace said, sniffling. She was pretty sure she had no tears left in her after last night.

"Because you cannot fix it by yourself, you think there is no solution. But you are wrong," Aunt Hester stated firmly. "You are overlooking two important things. The first " she said, lifting her index finger, "is that you think by leaving my nephew it will allow him to become the man he wants to be"—Grace nodded as she spoke—"but my dear, that man is hopelessly in love with you, and he will not realize his full potential without you by his side. If you leave him now, he will never accomplish anything he hopes to because he will be too broken to care." Feeling a tear slip down her cheek, Grace realized she could still cry.

"Second," the dowager continued, lifting another finger, "you are discounting the number of people moving within society who already support you and will speak on your behalf. Your friends the Earl and Countess of Geffen, the new Earl of Weston, members of Parliament from well-respected and titled families, and myself. You forget that I was a duchess for just over twenty years, and I wield quite the influence over many wives in the *ton*. If I spread word of my acceptance of you, they will fall in line. I'm sorry I did not state my support sooner so that you could think of this solution yourself," she finished with a smile.

Speechless, Grace looked at Aunt Hester as she wiped her cheeks. Finally, she asked, "Do you really think it could work?"

"I do." The dowager spoke with complete confidence. "Now will you please go and put my dear nephew out of his misery and assure him that you are staying and that you love him?"

Grace burst into laughter, all the tension of the past several days flooding out of her as a new path forward emerged. She was on the edge of hysteria as she swung between mirthful laughter and relieved sobs. She knew it would not be easy, but if Henry was willing to stay in the fight and if they had Aunt Hester on their side, Grace finally believed they would be able to create a place for themselves in polite society and enact the kinds of change they both desired. "I have to go and find Henry," she said.

"I whole heartedly agree, but let's make you a little more presentable first, don't you think?" Aunt Hester gestured to Grace's disheveled appearance in the mirror before calling for Lucy, and together they picked out one of Grace's new dresses and cleaned up her face.

With a renewed surge of energy, she raced toward the door. Upon opening it, she almost ran directly into Henry, who stood on the other side with his hand poised to knock. "Grace!" he exclaimed, grabbing her so she wouldn't stumble over.

"I was just going to look for you," she said, not quite sure how to begin.

"And I was coming to get you," he said.

They stood there for a moment looking at one another, before simultaneously attempting to utter apologies, stumbling over each other's words in the process.

"I'm so sorr…"

"I was a fool…"

Both stopped, Henry chuckling nervously and

Grace blushing. Finally, she leaned forward, wrapping her arms around him, and Henry immediately reciprocated. It felt like coming home. "Oh, Henry," she sighed.

He leaned down and kissed the top of her head, a simple sign of affection he had done so many times before. "I love you," he said into her hair. "I'm sorry I didn't tell you last night." He pulled away from her enough to look at her while not letting her out of his embrace. "I made a muddle of things because I was too shocked by your admission to express my own feelings." Brushing a stray lock of hair off her temple, he gazed at her with a look so full of love she thought it might melt her. "I wasn't trying to dismiss your concerns last night when I said that being able to enact change didn't matter. What I was trying to say was that while those things do matter, they don't matter to me nearly as much as you do."

It was all too much. Grace's heart was too full. She hadn't thought anything could top this day, but his admission of love made it perfect.

"I told you before," Henry continued, "that I will always care for and protect those I have chosen, but that it means more when they choose you back. I can't thank you enough for choosing me, too. None of this means anything if I don't have you to share it with. Please don't leave me. I can't be the man I want to be, the man you've shown me that I can be, without you."

"I'm not going to leave you," she choked out, aware that she was crying again. "I'm so sorry that I didn't fight harder for you. I thought I was doing what was best. I'll always want the best for you because I do love you, Henry. I love you so, so much."

He held her face tenderly as he gave her the sweetest, most perfect kiss, and Grace felt like she could breathe again. She could feel his love pouring into her through his kiss, and she wasn't sure how she had ever doubted his feelings.

He pulled away and rested his forehead against hers. "As much as I would love to stay just like this all day," he murmured with closed eyes, "I have made some changes that I need to tell you about." Straightening back up and opening his eyes, he took her hand. "Follow me downstairs?"

Leading her down the hallway, they descended the main stairs until reaching the grand foyer where the entire staff was assembled. "Henry," she said, pulling gently on his hand to stop him before they reached their audience, "what's going on?"

"I need to apologize to you, Grace," he said. "I know how much it meant to you to have a place in your own home and to run the manor as duchess. That has been hampered lately, and I know you've felt frustrated and undermined. I didn't support you the way I should have, but that ends now."

Turning back toward the group of servants who were eager to know why they had been called from their work, he pulled her forward until they were standing at the edge of the gathering and everyone could see them.

"Thank you all for taking time out of your work today to gather as I requested. I wanted to let you all know of some changes that will be happening in the household, including a few staff transitions," Henry announced. Grace was curious what he meant about staff changes but held her tongue as he continued. She noticed that Aunt Hester had also come downstairs and was listening from behind them.

"There has been quite a bit of transition in this house within the past year. It cannot be easy for many of you to have adjusted to the idea of a new duke right after my cousin had married and provided you with a new duchess. I know many of you watched him grow up here and feel his loss just as my aunt and I do. You have been patient with me this past year as I have learned as much as I could regarding the estate and what now falls under my mantle of responsibility. More change came when I unexpectedly presented you with a new duchess." He turned and smiled at Grace, squeezing the hand he still held. "It's never easy learning to report to a new mistress, but I was happy with how quickly you all welcomed her and responded to her ideas. Make no mistake, my wife has my full confidence in her abilities to lead this household, and she is unequivocally in charge." Henry paused to look around the room and make sure his words were understood.

"To make sure there is no confusion in that regard, my aunt, the dowager duchess, has arranged to move her residence over to the Dower House. As a longtime, faithful servant to her during her tenure as duchess, Standish will be accompanying her. James has agreed to step up from his current position of underbutler and will be taking over as butler until full staff decisions can be made. Thank you, James."

Grace couldn't believe what she was hearing. She turned and looked at Aunt Hester, who smiled at her in a way that let her know all had been settled beforehand.

"If any of you have questions about these changes, you can ask me or Mrs. Green," Henry said. "Just one more thing before you all go. Mrs. Nelsen?"

"Yes, Your Grace," the cook responded apprehensively.

"Would it be too much trouble for you and your staff to begin preparing individual plates for breakfast again, rather than a buffet?" Henry politely requested.

Smiling wide, Mrs. Nelson replied, "It would be my pleasure, Your Grace."

CHAPTER 38

Leading Grace out to the garden, Henry stopped when they reached a rosebush.

"What is this?" she asked, "these roses weren't here before."

"No, we didn't have any roses in the garden here at the manor, so I asked our gardener to plant some. I wanted to make sure you had a place you could come when you were tired, worried, or happy, so you could always smell the scent that you love the most. I hope they can bring you peace and joy, or whatever you might need in that moment." He looked at her fondly as she leaned over and took a deep sniff of one of the fully opened, cream-colored roses. She had become so precious to him, and he didn't know why he hadn't recognized sooner that his feelings had grown from deep affection to love.

"Thank you," she said, straightening up and placing her hand in the crook of his arm. "Henry, when did you ask the gardener to find the roses?"

"As soon as we arrived back here at the manor and I realized none were included in the garden. Why do you ask?"

"It's just a very thoughtful and romantic gesture. I've been wondering how long your feelings for me have grown past those of a marriage of convenience." Holding up a rose, she said, "This shows we may have been fooling ourselves from the beginning."

"I may have been a bit of a fool who didn't realize I had fallen in love with you until last night, but from the moment I proposed we marry to help one another, I always felt affection for you." Henry had always struggled to find the right words to express how he felt, but he wanted her to know that she mattered. He had tried to show her with gestures, and it seemed the roses were working, but he needed to find the words as well. He began to guide her down the garden path so they could walk and take in the air.

"I had a long talk with my aunt last night, and she apologized for making things more difficult for us by trying to help in such an unstraightforward manner. She really has come to care for you, and she only challenged you so much because she wanted to help you claim your confidence."

"She explained some of that to me this morning," Grace said. "I do appreciate she was trying to help, but I really do wish she had gone about it another way."

Henry smiled at her diplomatic answer. "Yes. I think all involved believe that. Poor Lord Camden most especially."

"Thank you for so firmly putting your support

behind me with the staff this morning." She paused for a moment, and he could see she was gathering her thoughts. Continuing to walk again, he realized that silences never felt uncomfortable with her and he had no urge to fill the gap in conversation. "I've always thought that women are just as strong as men, only in different ways. For a long time, I was denied my own agency, and when I had the chance to start fresh here, I wanted to be able to show what I was capable of and do it on my own. I think part of my frustration recently has been because I felt I wasn't able to handle things independently, and I resented things might be easier if you were to step in and advocate on my behalf."

Henry could tell it was hard for her to make that admission. "Grace, I never for a moment thought you were not qualified to do everything you wished to. I'm sorry I did not stand up for you sooner, but only because I think it might have made things easier if everyone knew we were a team, not because I don't think you are capable. Aunt Hester helped me understand last night that I might have been too hasty to disregard some of your concerns and that we can work to overcome any challenges together."

"I'm sorry that I couldn't see past my own fears to recognize that we could strengthen each other," she said. "You truly see me, Henry. Knowing that you understand who I am and choose me anyway, even with all my faults, makes me feel more powerful than I ever would be alone." Grace stopped walking and turned toward him. Lifting her hands to cup his face, she raised up on her toes and pulled him in for a kiss.

"I love you, Henry. Thank you for everything. I've felt lost for a very long time, needing to hide to protect myself. But your belief in me has helped me to find my true self again. The security and love you provide me make me feel safe enough to explore what truly matters to me again."

Overcome by her words, he gathered her in his arms and showed her how treasured she was with another kiss. He intended to be gentle, but his desire for her was overwhelming and the kiss became ravenous. He was heartened by the fact that Grace was attacking him with an equal amount of fervor. He couldn't stop his hands from running over her body and pulled her in as close as possible. The need to consume her was irresistible, and he wasn't sure he could hold himself back if she didn't stop him.

Finally, the need for air outweighed anything else and they separated with a gasp. Still clinging to him, as if she wasn't sure she could support herself, Grace suggested maybe they should head back toward the house. "I'm not sure a ravishing in the garden is the best place for us to come together again," she said with a glint in her eye. Henry did not need to be told twice, and they turned around and set off for the manor.

"When will your aunt be moving to the Dower House?" Grace asked, a welcome distraction so he could try and calm himself from the earlier inferno they had created. "That announcement was quite a surprise this morning."

"Soon," he reassured her. "I should have asked her to transition there as soon as she arrived back, but I thought I would need her around to help me gain confidence in my role. I struggle when I am not able to do things well, and I felt I needed her until I was comfortable as the duke. I didn't think about how that might make things awkward for both of you as you adjusted to new roles and positions. I was so concerned about you feeling confident in taking over the house that I failed to realize it may be hard for her to let go as well. It was actually her idea last night that she should make the move sooner rather than later."

"And Standish?" Grace asked.

"I had a talk with him early this morning and he apologized for continuing to regard the dowager as mistress of the house. Knowing he was close to my aunt, I proposed he move to the Dower House with her, and he happily agreed."

"I'll have to thank your aunt," she said. "It seems like things just might work out after all."

When they returned to the house, Grace's plans to fully reconnect with her husband were upended when they found things in an uproar. Lord Camden was now awake and, though perfectly recovered, was raging about how he had been intentionally poisoned the night before.

"This is an absolute disgrace, and I will not submit to being treated with such disrespect! Where is His Grace? I demand to speak to him at once!" They followed the sounds of his diatribe to the front hallway, where they saw Camden perched on the stairs, screaming at a stoic Standish.

Noticing they had come back, Standish addressed them. "Ah, Your Grace," he said with a bow.

"It seems Lord Camden wishes to have a word with you."

"Yes, my lord?" Henry said with a straight face as he turned toward a sputtering Camden.

"I have never been treated with such disrespect in my life!" Camden repeated, purple with feigned rage. "What do you have to say for yourself, and how do you plan to make this up to me?" Once again, he made his plan to try and gain the favor of a duke perfectly plain with his statement. Grace and Henry, however, now a united front, would not be easily swayed.

"I do sincerely apologize, my lord," Grace said with a smile, trying to appeal to his vanity. "I'm afraid there was a mix up with the meal last night. I was aware of your sensitivity to nuts, so I had asked our cook to prepare the fish with lemon sauce. Apparently, when she did not have enough lemons for the preparation, she sought out a solution by changing to the preparation with almonds. I was not aware of the change, so I was unable to stop it from being served. I can assure you that it was an unfortunate mistake. Please do accept my apology."

"Your apology means nothing," Camden shouted. "What kind of a duchess are you if you don't even know what is going on in your own household?" Where once such a statement would have stung, Grace had renewed confidence in her position with Henry by her side, as he squeezed her hand in silent support, allowing her to take the lead.

"I'm afraid that was my fault," Standish interjected, surprising all of them. "I was unable to find Her Grace and went to the dowager duchess for approval of the menu change. Unfortunately, the dowager was unaware of your allergy. She is most regretful that you were indisposed." Grace gave Standish the full wattage of her smile.

"The whole lot of you are incapable. I'll make sure the entirety of the *ton* knows how ill I've been treated here." Camden refused to let go of the high ground he seemed to think he had gained overnight, but he didn't realize his threats no longer intimidated either her or Henry.

"Feel free to do your worst," Henry said. "It was an unfortunate incident but should make a charming and humorous anecdote for you someday soon." How he managed to say that with a straight face was beyond Grace's comprehension.

"No one will ever take either of you seriously. It's clear this entire marriage is a complete farce. I always knew you were an ungrateful social climber," Camden directed at Grace with a sneer.

"And what does that make you?" Grace asked him. "You're the one who came crawling here to claim a relationship to me now that I outrank you, when previously you disregarded me. It seems you are the one currently seeking to elevate himself through thinly veiled blackmail based on an unintentional circumstance." Camden spluttered while Henry beamed in approval.

"I can assure you," Henry said, bringing Grace in even closer to his side, "this is most certainly not anything other than a very real and very loving marriage. There is no way for you to win here. What I told you yesterday still stands. I will not speak ill of you, nor will I claim any kind of relationship to you moving forward." Turning toward the butler, Henry said, "Standish, will you please show our guest out and make sure he is seen safely to the road?" Standish bowed in acknowledgment, and Henry calmly walked Grace upstairs past an enraged Camden. They ignored his continued blustering as they ascended the stairs, too caught up in one another.

Arriving at their bedchamber, the events of the past twenty-four hours were catching up with Grace and she found herself flagging. Henry noticed she was starting to drag and suggested she lay down for a while.

Starting to blush, she looked up at him shyly through her lashes. "I had hoped we might be able to spend some time together," she said. Henry grinned at her, understanding what she was intimating, but he simply leaned forward and kissed her forehead.

"I know, sweetheart," he said, using the endearment for the first time. "I'll be here ready and waiting for you when you wake up, but it's important for you to take care of yourself."

"What about you?" she asked him. "You must've hardly slept last night either—why don't you come and lie down with me?"

"That sounds like heaven," he responded. "There is nothing I like quite so much as having you in my arms."

Henry followed her into her room and helped her remove her dress so she would be able to sleep more comfortably before tucking her beneath the covers. Once he had also settled into the bed beside her, she nestled into his side and quite promptly fell asleep.

A few hours later, she awakened to find Henry still asleep. Grace took the time to simply drink in the sight of him, peaceful and at rest. He was so beautiful to her, inside and out. He showed her a level of care and respect she had never felt from anyone outside of her father. She felt like the luckiest woman in the world to be able to share her life with him and would do everything in her power to help him achieve his goals. Leaning forward, she placed a gentle kiss on his lips, and he stirred awake.

"That's a lovely way to wake up," he mumbled, smiling. He stretched his arms above his head and then turned back toward her to look at her fully. Reaching out to cup her cheek, he said, "I think I could get used to this."

"Me too," Grace assured him. "And we have the rest of our lives to do so." Enveloped in her husband's arms, she knew there was no place she would rather be.

EPILOGUE

LONDON- MARCH 1820

Grace took a deep breath and clutched Henry's hand as he helped her out of the carriage. She was about to attend the first formal event of the social season as the Duchess of Carrington. While still a bit trepidatious as to how she would be received, she was more concerned about what the ball would be like rather than how others would perceive her. But she had Henry by her side, and that was all that mattered.

Much had happened over the past six months as she and Henry had settled into their life together at Highland Manor. Not long after what came to be known as "the event" with Lord Camden, Aunt Hester had moved to the Dower House, allowing Henry and Grace some much needed space to breathe and leaving Grace the mistress of the house. She had made a few additional changes as to how things were run around the manor, but she still maintained many of the traditions she learned about from the dowager.

Aunt Hester had continued to school both her and

Henry on what to expect from the *ton* and shared many of the unwritten rules everyone followed. She was also happier now that she was living in the Dower House, as she was still close to the home she had lived in for many years but also had her own space to work through her grief. She enjoyed having her own domain once again and being able to tell Standish what to do. Grace had grown extremely fond of the older woman once they had cleared the air and come to an understanding about her role within the family. Grace valued her experience and wisdom, even if she did occasionally ignore her aunt's advice in favor of a new way of doing things.

Henry had come into his own as the duke, finally feeling confident in taking charge now that he had the help and support of his beloved wife. He had made many improvements around the estate and modernized farming techniques wherever possible. He took the time to gather input from the tenants, ensuring any changes he made were in their best interest and with their blessing. And he continued to spoil Grace with books and brought her dahlias as the summer transitioned into fall.

Their friends and the dowager had worked hard to raise intrigue about the new Duchess of Carrington, showering praise on her to those who would ask questions about the mystery woman who had managed to snag a duke. Grace was also less concerned about her reception in the *ton* because of the way Henry had already made a name for himself. The previous November, a special session of Parliament was called in response to the events over the summer, including the Peterloo Massacre. Taking up his seat in the House of Lords for the first time, Henry won the respect of many of his peers, even though he was a member of the more liberal Whig party. This would no doubt help with the opinions of the wives of the *ton*, as their husbands discussed the merits of the new duke.

His hard work and dedication to finding solutions that would benefit everyone within England garnered him the respect of men from all walks of life.

And now they were finally here, the first official event of the season, and Grace was more confident than ever. She had found a peace and strength in herself after feeling lost for so long. Knowing who she was, she no longer feared how the *ton* may judge her. She also knew Henry loved her, and that was enough.

Moira would be here this evening, ready to stand by her, and Angeline would also be attending her first seasonal event since losing her husband. Henry had also informed her that the young woman from Reid's estate who had so captured his attention would be re-entering society this evening, and Grace was eager to make her acquaintance. In the end, it didn't matter if there were whispers about the new duchess and her unusual relationship to high society. She was surrounded by those who loved and supported her just as she was, and that was all she needed. With her head held high, she walked into the ballroom on the arm of her husband and went to find their friends.

RUIN AND REDEMPTION FOR THE EARL

Ruin and Redemption for the Earl is the second book in the Reluctant Lords series.

She believed herself to be ruined, and he didn't care

Ruined in the eyes of polite society for breaking one of the unspoken rules of the *ton,* Lady Elise Pelham has had to make a life for herself in a world that is not easy for a single woman to navigate on her own. All she desires is to be able to live life on her own terms, embracing the freedom she now has without the shackles of propriety.

Returning to his family's estate on the Dorset Coast, Reid Claybourn, the new Earl of Weston, wants to do anything other than take over the title. Resentful that he must now relinquish his influential place in the House of Commons to take up his seat in the House of Lords, he is struggling to find his place as the earl.

When Reid and Elise meet on his estate, the attraction between them is immediate. But will Elise be able to let go of the comfortable world she has created for herself in order to be with Reid? And can Reid find a way to embrace his new place in the peerage if he does not have Elise beside him?

ACKNOWLEDGMENTS

Publishing this book is literally a dream come true, and it would not have been possible without the support of many people.

Thank you goes first and foremost to my dad, who has been an unwavering support through this entire process. My sister has also been my constant cheerleader, and their belief in me has sustained me and made this change in my life possible.

The support from the rest of my extended family and close friends has been overwhelming. Deciding to leave a 15-year career in student and academic development in higher education was scary, but you never questioned my pivot and supported my crazy idea to try and write for a living.

Learning how to navigate the world of self-publishing has been quite the journey, and it wouldn't have been possible without many people to help me along the way:

Jennifer Prokop, thank you for your willingness to work with an unknown author. Your support has helped me keep faith in myself, and my stories are infinitely better for your suggestions. I can't imagine having done this without you!

Nick Shea, thank you for your endless patience with me and your excellent copyedits. You helped me write the story I wanted to tell in a cleaner and more straightforward manner.

Erin Dameron-Hill—where do I even start. I cannot stop gushing to everyone about how gorgeous the covers you created are! Seeing this first cover completed made me feel like a real author, and it provides a level of professionalism to the book.

Alaina and Maureen, thank you for being willing to read my *very* rough first drafts and give me feedback. Talking through the stories with you has been invaluable, and I am so grateful for your interest and belief in me!

And finally, thanks to *you*—my readers! An author is nothing without people who read and enjoy their stories. I hope you will continue on this journey with me.

ALSO BY ANDIE JAMES

The Reluctant Lords Series

Lost and Found by the Duke

Ruin and Redemption for the Earl

Once and Again with the Viscount

For a short story about how Moira and Fitz met and fell in love, sign up for my newsletter at
<u>andiejamesauthor.com/contact</u>

Available exclusively to those on my mailing list.

ABOUT THE AUTHOR

Andie James is an emerging author of historical romance books. This is Andie's first book.

Though a voracious reader her entire life, it wasn't until more recently Andie truly fell in love with romance. During the pandemic, she needed something lighter and joyful—and the HEA in romance fit the bill. Focusing on historical romance, Andie loves the element of fantasy inherent to the genre, and the way a historical lens can provide new ways to understand contemporary issues.

Andie happily lives in Tacoma, WA with her cat. There is nothing she enjoys more than curling up with a good book and coffee. Fulfilled by good food and time with loved ones, she appreciates a good story in any form (book, movie, theatre, NPR reporting), and tries to live by the philosophy of Ted Lasso.

andiejamesauthor.com

facebook.com/100093985703609
twitter.com/andiejauthor
instagram.com/andiejamesauthor

Made in United States
Troutdale, OR
07/26/2023

11544330R00202